MW01601982

ghosted

je rowney

Also by this author

Charcoal

Derelict

PROLOGUE

Have you ever had a friend who you do absolutely everything with? Do people refer to you as 'joined at the hip' or wonder if your relationship runs to more than just friendship? She's been married for five years and you have a long-term boyfriend, but people like to talk.

You were her bridesmaid of course. She had the perfect wedding, while you had a series of unfortunate relationships before meeting The One. She reminds you that he is not actually The One, and on some level, you suspect she may be correct. You discuss this less often than you used to because you work shifts as a midwife and she's a high school teacher now. Grown up jobs. Sometimes you can't quite believe it.

Even though you feel she is more successful than you, with the perfect home, perfect family, you're not jealous. How could you be? She's Zoe. She's your best friend. You've known her for twenty-two years, and as you've only been alive for twenty-five years, that's going to be hard to beat.

You're Violet and Zoe. Your names can't be combined in one of those cool 'Brangelina' ways, but you have been friends way longer than that relationship lasted, and you spent many nights over many glasses of Prosecco, gossiping about how you always knew he should have stayed with Aniston. Ziolet. Voe. Neither works. On paper perhaps your friendship shouldn't work either.

She's a petite redhead whose parents were quite something in the 1960s. You have a vague idea of what that means. You know it involved being in the right place at the right time with the right people, hanging with the in-crowd, taking too many drugs. It doesn't appear to have done any damage to anyone.

Meanwhile, your parents are a forklift truck driver and a sales assistant at Wilko. At least your dad was a forklift truck driver last time you heard from him but that was eight years ago. You inherited your work ethic from your mother and your gangly legs and mud-brown hair from your father.

Zoe tells you that she wishes she were as tall and *exotic* as you are, but you fail to see much exotic about having grown up on a council estate in Creekmoor. You were the first from your family to go to university, and you scraped by with a 2:2 while you watched Zoe graduate with a first-class degree. You knew that she would, and you're proud of her, but she is just as proud of you. She knows about the relationship you went through while you were trying to study. She knows about the guy who seemed so perfect, but ended up being anything but. She knows how much it means to you that you managed to get through university at all. She knows that you don't want to talk about him, that you don't even want to think about him now that you have moved on to better things.

You are Violet and Zoe. You don't know what you would do without her. Without Zoe, you are 'Violet and'. You are missing a piece. When you ask her "What would I do without you?", she tells you that you'll never have to be. But what if that's not true? What if one day she's just not there anymore?

CHAPTER ONE

"If you don't want to go..."

Adrian cuts me off before I get the end of the sentence.

"How do you think it makes me look if you message half an hour before we are supposed to be there and say we aren't going?"

"I can say I have a migraine. Or..."

"You used that one last time. Zoe isn't stupid. Do you think she's stupid? Is your friend stupid?"

He drags the word out in a protracted drawl. Stooopid. It curdles in the air between us.

"Of course not."

I'm trying to get ready whilst having this conversation. Adrian is sitting on our bed, still dressed in the jeans and lame cartoon print T-shirt combo that he's been wearing all day. We are mismatched. I thought I'd wear something special, even though it's only dinner and drinks at my best friend's house. Opportunities to dress up don't seem to come around often enough. I chose a black jersey cotton knee-length dress, plain and pretty. I suppose it's casual enough to match his outfit, if I don't wear the pendant necklace and I tone down my make-up. I've paused in front of the mirror while I consider these things.

"Is this okay?" I ask, turning over my shoulder to look at him. He's lying back on to the bed now, not even looking at me.

"You look fine," he says robotically, still staring at the ceiling.

I think about asking him if he's going to get changed, but we only have ten minutes before we need to set off, and that's not long enough for an argument.

"We can leave early." It's the best I can think of.

He waves his hand, as though swatting away a fly that's irritating him.

I spray a little grapefruit cologne onto my pulse points, and head over to join him.

"I hate that one," he says, shuffling away from me as I curl in next to him.

"What?"

"That perfume. I hate it."

"It's the Jo Mason. You bought it for me."

I see his face change momentarily. There's a tiny flicker of recognition, and I know that he knows I'm right.

"Not that one," he says. "I wouldn't have bought you that. It smells slutty."

It's a £100 bottle of perfume. It was a present from Adrian to me on our eighteen-month anniversary, which was only two months ago. It's not cheap, and I believe it's widely agreed that it is not slutty. How does something even smell 'slutty' anyway? I can't ask, and I know that pointing out his mistake won't lead to anything good, so I say, "I must be wrong." I'm careful to keep my tone flat and genuine. I know it could come across as sarcasm if I don't keep myself in check.

I put my arm around him in a placatory gesture, but he wriggles further away, petulantly.

"You must be," he says. "Wash it off."

I look at my watch. I'm one of those old school types who likes to wear a wristwatch even though I carry my phone everywhere. It's almost time to leave.

"If we are late, we are late," he says. I know he doesn't mean it. If we are late, he will be livid.

Without arguing, I push myself up off the bed and head to the bathroom. I run a flannel under the tap and feel the warmth of the water on my hands. The woman in the mirror above the sink looks at me.

"It's fine," I tell her. "It's only perfume. It's fine."

Her expression tells me that she doesn't really think it's 'fine'. I look away, squeeze out the flannel and press the cloth to my neck, wiping away at the place where I sprayed the sweet citrus scent. The cotton feels good against my skin, like a warm kiss. I rub gently, right round to the back of my neck, massaging away the pent-up tension. Mirror-me watches.

"Remember when he used to kiss you there?"

I touch the place where my artery pulsates. I remember. The woman looks at me with the sadness of someone who has lost something important but isn't quite sure what it is. I look away to wash my hands, clean my wrists, make myself more desirable. Less undesirable. I'm not sure which.

I hadn't planned on drinking tonight but maybe I'll have a glass of wine or two.

"Are you ready?"

9

Am I? I'm not even sure of that.

We arrive at Zoe and Luke's house at five past eight. I'm not usually bothered about exact timing when it's just me and her, but Adrian is anal about punctuality. If we say we will be somewhere at a certain time he gets twitchy if we are late.

"Sorry," he says to Luke, before Zoe's husband has time to say hello. "Missy here was dragging her feet, couldn't decide what to wear. You know how it is with these girls."

Girls. Sometimes when a man calls you a 'girl' it's a compliment, or you can choose to take it as one. It's a marker of youth. Arguably it's a marker of immaturity. My dad used to refer to mum and me as 'you girls' and it felt like she and I were a team, a little unit. It was a bonding term, and the feeling that I got when he spoke those words was warm, like a hug. Until things started to sour between my parents, that is. Once their relationship began to crumble, the semantics of our family also fell apart. 'You girls' became a criticism, a caution. 'You girls' are lazy. 'You girls' should try harder. 'You girls' are a waste of my time. Eventually,

10

of course, he left us girls, and we were, in our isolation, we girls. When Adrian says 'these girls', I know it's the sour, not the sweet. It feels more like sandpaper than silk. But Zoe and I are a unit, just as mum and I were, as mum and I still are on some level.

I smile dumbly, and say hello, give a little half hug and kiss to the cheek.

"Alright," Luke says to us both. "No damage done. Come on through. Drinks guys?"

Adrian asks for a beer and I work out that I'll be the designated driver tonight. It's fine. I hardly drink when I'm out with him. That wine that I wanted can wait.

I nod at him and say that I'll have a diet cola. All good. Much better for me. My choice earns me a gleaming smile from Adrian. Much better for me.

Zoe makes a little excited squeaking noise when she sees me, and I notice Adrian rolling his eyes towards Luke, trying to get him on side. 'The boys' are just being boys, or at least Adrian is being a boy, and Luke is being polite. To Adrian. Zoe and I hug, then she steps back and looks at my clothes.

"You look amazing," she says. "I should have made more of an effort. I've been in the kitchen all evening though."

I believe her. She always goes so over the top about these dinners. Three courses, all homemade from scratch, always incredible. I wave away her compliment.

"You don't have to. You're always spot on, Zo."

She's wearing a green tunic dress, about two tones darker than her eyes. She bought it last time we went shopping together in town. She's one of those women (you girls) that knows exactly what suits her and never has to even try anything on in the shops. I go from store to store collecting armfuls of outfits, none of which end up being any good. I'm too misshapen, too awkward, too insecure in my own skin. Zoe is effortless.

"Do you need any help with anything?"

The men have gone through to the lounge, while we stand in the hallway between entrance and kitchen. Rich meaty aromas float from the oven. I didn't know how hungry I was until the scent struck me. Now I'm near drooling.

"I'm fine, everything is under control. Come and talk to me while I finish up. Unless you'd rather..." She gestures through the living room door, where I can see Adrian taking control of the remote and browsing through to the football.

"I'll come with you, thanks," I say, and I take a seat at the breakfast bar.

She kicks the door shut and we have a few minutes of seclusion away from 'the boys'.

"Everything okay?" She speaks to me in a low whisper, as though we are inmates hatching a plot against our gaolers.

"Yeah. Sure. Nothing new," I say.

"Hmm. That's not necessarily a good thing."

"Everything is fine. At the moment."

She knows how it is. God knows we have talked about it often enough. Over wine, over latte, on the sofa, in bars, in coffee shops. We have talked and talked. Sometimes I just don't want to talk any more.

"What about you?" I ask. I know I'm deflecting, and so does she, but she raises an eyebrow and answers.

"Actually, I..."

But then our quiet time ends abruptly. The door judders open. It's Luke.

"Drinks," he says. "I forgot. Adrian's acting like his throat's been cut."

He sticks his head in the fridge and clatters the bottles.

Whatever Zoe was going to say is now lost, the moment has passed. She waves the thought away and prods at whatever is in the pan. I throw her a questioning look, but she shakes her head and gestures towards the fridge, to Luke. You know what these girls are like with their secrets.

Ten minutes later and we are sitting at the pine country-kitchen-style dining table. I think Zoe would have been happy leaving town and settling down in a barn conversion out in west Dorset. White cliffs, stormy seas, home-made apple pies and cider. I could see her apron-clad, rosy-cheeked. Smiling. Not that she's

14

not happy here. We live by the sea, in a town that is full of tourists in the summer, and students and elderly the rest of the year. It's not a bad place to be.

Zoe has fallen into a perfect relationship with a perfect man. She might not describe her teaching job as perfect, but I've seen the way her eyes shine when she tells me about how she's supporting some troubled kid, about how he's achieving more than she ever imagined. More than he ever believed. I've heard the pride in her voice, and I've felt proud for her achievements too. When she succeeds, I feel a glow, not the pangs of jealousy.

I realise I'm staring at her, but at least I'm smiling.

"You okay, Vi?" she mouths, silently.

I nod. It seems like she asks me that a lot recently. Way too often. Not that I don't appreciate the way that she cares, the way that she looks out for me, of course I do. I appreciate it so much. I appreciate her so much.

Adrian is oblivious to our exchange. He's focussed on spooning mash onto his plate from the serving dish, heaping high the fluffy, buttery clouds. I'll just have a little. I'm trying to cut down on my carbs. As I think this, I'm suddenly aware of the way that my belly bulges in this dress when I sit, so I pull myself closer to the table to hide it.

"Looks great, Zo. Thanks for doing this."

"Tuck in, I don't want any leftovers, or I'll just be picking at them when you've gone home. Get some of that on your plate."

She leans across the table and spoons a huge dollop of cauliflower cheese next to my chicken fillet. I think that I'd better skip the mash altogether, but as soon as Adrian puts the serving spoon down, Zoe's passing the bowl over to me.

"Easy on that, Violet," Adrian says.

I put my hand onto my belly in a reflex action, feeling the flab, feeling so self-conscious.

Zoe tuts and shakes her head, not even bothering to rise to the comment. It wasn't aimed at her. Her with her perfect, petite figure. She's always been a size eight, super slim, petite and perfect. I've always struggled to stay at a size fourteen never mind lose weight and be any smaller. I'm a good five inches taller than her, so my weight is dispersed, but...

"Don't listen to him," she says. "Enjoy yourself."

It's difficult not to listen to something that you hear all the time. A dripping tap becomes more irritating the longer it plink-plinks away. Chinese water torture, that's what it is. The constant drops of words that fall upon my ears, wearing away at me, eroding my confidence.

I accept a small portion of potatoes, but I'm already planning not to eat them.

We eat, we talk, and we laugh. I relax into the evening, and Adrian is too consumed by what he is consuming to needle me for a while. Of course, it's short-lived.

"It's the gin festival at the end of the month, Vi," Zoe says.

"Oh mate, yes! That's come around quickly. Bloody hell!"

"A whole year since Knickergate!"

Adrian nudges me.

"What's 'Knickergate'? I don't think I've heard about this?"

Zoe starts to tell the story, even though I am shaking my head, signalling at her to stop.

"So, the festival is in Baiter Park, the one near the harbour."

Adrian nods. He's stopped eating, set his cutlery down by his plate, giving this conversation his complete attention. It's already unnerving me.

"There's all these little stalls with amazing gins. Rhubarb, orange, toffee apple," she continues, pulling her face at the last flavour. "The idea is that you're meant to buy some, of course, but they give out loads of free samples, so we were half-cut before we'd even been there an hour. Then this one…" She points at me. "This one decides she needs to pee."

"We're eating, Zoe!" Luke says. Adrian gestures at her to carry on with the tale.

"There were these Porta-Potties. Those green plastic disgusting…" She pauses again, looks at the food. "Maybe I'll tell you about this later instead." She laughs.

Adrian does not laugh. Adrian's face is deadpan. "No. Carry on."

I see Zoe pass a quick glance to Luke, but he's not looking at her, he's shovelling mash towards his mouth.

Zoe gives a short sigh and continues, less enthusiastically.

"Violet went into one of them, did her thing, and managed to come out with her skirt tucked into her knickers. She was wearing this really cute red flowery skirt, but it's all, you know, loose and billowy." She moves her arms to indicate the flapping of the dress. "The funny thing was neither of us noticed. So this couple were looking at her and nudging each other, laughing, and she was like 'what the fuck?' and we were so drunk that we didn't even…anyway eventually this old guy taps her on the shoulder and I was thinking like 'uh-oh, here comes some drunk trying his luck' He says 'excuse me love' and points at her bottom. She's all outraged and 'excuse ME'. Of course, he's not at all drunk and he tells her that she's flashing everyone, and she turns as red as that skirt. Then we laughed and laughed and, oh God, it was hilarious."

I'm guffawing, trying to hold in the full-blown booming laugh that wants to come out. Then I look at Adrian. He is still stony-faced. I feel like I've just swallowed a bowling ball.

"And when is this festival?"

His tone has changed. He doesn't have the air of light inquisitiveness any longer, it's changed to something more serious, and I'm not sure where this line of enquiry is heading.

Zoe hasn't picked up on the switch and she continues.

"Er, twenty-seventh, twenty-eighth."

"Which?"

His question is terse, abrupt. Something almost imperceptible flashes across Zoe's face that lets me know that she feels the change too, like a dark cloud creeping into a previously clear blue sky.

"Both," she says. Her voice is firm and steady. "It's a two-day festival. Music. Alcohol. Fun."

"We do it every year," I say. My voice is less steady than Zoe's. "It's like a tradition."

"Traditional drinking?

"Traditional fun. It's our Girls Weekend," Zoe answers him, and I'm glad she does until she adds,

"And nothing comes between us and our Girls Weekend."

At this, Luke laughs and stands up.

"I wouldn't dare, Zo. On the subject of traditional drinks, I see some empty glasses at this table. Ladies? Adrian?"

Zoe and I pass our empties up to him, her wine glass and a tumbler for my cola, but Adrian is motionless. He could be made of marble: cold, silent, still.

"Mate?" Luke prompts him, but he still doesn't respond. "Drink?"

"Adrian?" I say. My voice is tiny and fragile. A speckled blue eggshell holding my thoughts, my feelings.

"That's the weekend I said that we would visit my mother," he says, eventually. It's the first I have heard of any plans or any visit. I want to say that we'll have to change the date, visit her another time, but I don't want to start that conversation here and now. I don't want to start that argument.

Luke raises his hands in a 'leave me out of it' gesture, and heads to the kitchen.

"You can visit her another time," Zoe says, and I wish so much that she didn't say it. I want to reach over and stuff those words back into her mouth. I want to rewind them, erase them.

I expect Adrian to lose it, but instead he smiles.

"Not possible, I'm afraid. It's been planned for some time. Violet must have forgotten about it, but it's a very special, important date for my mother and I really can't let her down."

At this I wrinkle my brow and try to search my memory for any trace of him having told me about a visit. I would have remembered a special date, wouldn't I? I would have remembered his mother. I try, I try some more, but nothing.

"I'm sorry," I say. "I can't believe I forgot." It's true. I can't believe I would forget. I don't quite believe that I have forgotten.

"Maybe you can visit your mother while Vi and I go to the festival?" Zoe keeps saying things that are not things that I want her to say.

"Maybe you can keep your stupid little thoughts to yourself," Adrian says, and now it's his words I want to delete. I'm thinking that I'm glad that Luke is out of the room, and I'm about to speak when I hear the words from the doorway.

"What did you just say?"

Luke is standing with a glass of wine in each hand and a face flushed with fury.

Oh God, this is it.

"Leave it," Zoe says, "I think Adrian might have had enough to drink now."

Apparently, you can make a bad situation worse.

Adrian stands up and I'm sure for a split second that he's going to reach across the table and slap Zoe. He's like a tightly coiled spring that's just been released. He leaps up, towering over the table. Luke drops the glasses, as if the carpet and the glassware are less important than the situation that's escalating.

"You'd better stop right there, mate." He moves up close to Adrian and now I'm almost certain that someone is going to be slapping someone. Or worse.

"Let's go," Adrian says, reaching down for my hand.

Normally, I would instantly slide my hand into his, following his instruction, but something keeps me firmly pressed into my seat.

I'm the driver. He's hardly going to leave without me.

"Let's. Go."

He punctuates the two words, emphasising his insistence. Still, I have no intention of getting up. I am in my safe place. Nothing bad can happen here, in front of Zoe and Luke.

I half expect Luke to say something else, but the two of them are dumbstruck now. It's like there's a digital timer on a bomb counting down between us, and if anyone moves or speaks it could trigger the explosion. I don't know which wire to cut. I don't know how to defuse this.

"Seriously, Violet."

He leans towards me, grabbing at me and I pull back so hard that I almost fall from my seat. Instead of feeling a slap, he's stuck his hand into my dress pocket, breathing his heavy breath into my face, pressing into me, making my head spin. I'm going to faint. I can feel the weightless whirr.

Luke leaps into action, yanking on Adrian's T-shirt, failing to get enough purchase to pull him off me, and scrabbling for his arm instead.

"Get the fuck off me," Adrian says. He barks the words like a rabid mutt, but he does stumble back, dangling the car keys he retrieved from my pocket.

"I'm leaving. You choose whether you're coming."

How many beers has he had? Two? Three? I look at Zoe, and she gives me a helpless shrug of her shoulders. She doesn't know how to stop this any more than I do. I don't want to go, but I don't want him to drive either. Not in this state, not like this.

"Okay," I say. "Okay." I nearly tell him to calm down, the words are forming, ready to pour out, but I stop myself. I know what effect they would have.

I pat my hands against the air, as though trying to soothe a rearing rodeo stallion. Woah. Woah boy.

Zoe grips my wrist as I walk past her, head bowed, following Adrian to the door.

"Text me when you get home." She says it in such an earnest tone that I just nod and pat her hand on my arm.

I mouth "I'm sorry" without saying the words out loud and she shakes her head, dismissing the apology as unnecessary.

Luke mutters something under his breath and I'm glad that I don't hear what it is, because that means that Adrian doesn't either.

I take a deep breath and let Adrian lead me out of the door.

I expect Adrian's anger to be aimed solely at me, but all I hear on the way home is a diatribe against Zoe and Luke.

"I don't know why you hang around with her. Trashy, gobby bitch."

"She's my friend, Adrian. She's always been my friend."

"That doesn't mean that she always has to be your friend. You can stop being friends. People change, move on, outgrow each other. Perhaps you've outgrown her."

I shake my head. I'm trying to concentrate on the road. It's dark, I'm shaking, I just want to be home.

"And Luke. The way he panders to her. It's gross."

He spits the word out like a bad tasting chunk of gristle.

"You're not going to that festival with her. No way."

I knew that was what sparked all this, and I know that he's been waiting to bring it up again. I am going. There's nothing that will stop me, not even him. This is going to be a problem. A bigger problem than it already is. I say nothing, I think many things.

"She's a bad influence. Bad, bad influence."

I hear the words and let them wash over me. I know when to argue back and I know when to bite my words and swallow them.

I sit in silence as I feign listening to him for the rest of the journey.

When we arrive home, he kisses me, as if everything is fine between us. Snap. Back to normal, as if nothing has happened.

"At least we got to come home early. Do you fancy watching a film or…?"

I know from his expression what the alternative that he's about the suggest is, and it sickens me to think of that right now. After the way he treated Zoe. After the way he treated me. It's the last thing on my mind

I raise my hand to my temple and flash a sad look.

"I have a bit of a headache actually. I might get changed and maybe have a lie down."

It's ten o'clock and I think I can probably go to bed and sleep until morning. Sleep through the aftermath of the evening's excitement.

He shrugs and heads into the living room. The idea was probably just 'something to do' for him. It's not always an intimate, emotional thing, but that doesn't mean that I don't *want* it to be intimate and emotional. I watch him walk away and then slip upstairs.

The tension hasn't spilled over into our home. It was going to go one or two ways. Either he was going to go off at me for the rest of the evening or he would retreat and move on. The worst part is that I never know what to expect. I'm never sure whether he's going to be lovable or loathsome.

I fall onto our bed   fully   clothed, feeling   the relief of being alone.

Later, when Adrian finally makes his way to bed and falls asleep, I lie in the darkness, eyes open, staring into the black. I listen to his breathing, the grumbling nasal inhalation, the rasping release. As my vision acclimatises to the lack of light, I can make out his outline in the bed beside me. The rise and fall of the cover over his contours. In the dimness, he is simply an object, a heavy weight. There was a time that I might have looked at him this way with affection. There was a time that I would have wanted him to awaken, to keep talking to me, to prolong the day. Now, I feel only glad that he is sleeping. As I watch him, the sensation I feel is one of relief, or relaxation, and something that at first, I can't put my finger on, but recognise as revulsion.

We have lived here together for the past five months. He pushed and pushed for me to move in with him. Why waste money on maintaining two homes when we could live together? Not the most romantic of reasons, but the practical seemed pragmatic.

This has to end. I have to end it.

CHAPTER TWO

Getting up for work the next morning is hell. I'm not a morning person at the best of times, but after the stress and sleeplessness, I'm a wreck. Of course, I'm rostered to work in theatre. It couldn't get much worse. The operating list starts at nine o'clock and I'll be on my feet until at least noon. The operating theatre is always hotter than regular room temperature, no windows, no air con. Dressed in scrubs, a surgical gown, cap and face mask, it feels stifling. I wear a clear plastic visor that covers my eyes, protects them from splashes, and it regularly steams up in the uncomfortable heat. Mostly, when we aren't between patients, in that blissful ten-minute turnaround time, I am wearing sterile non-latex gloves and I can't even wipe the hair from my brow when a random strand falls down. Everything is clean. Everything is controlled.

My shift starts at seven thirty, and there's an hour of prep to do before we start the list. I make sure we have enough theatre packs, the pre-wrapped collections of bowls, instruments, swabs and gauzes that we need for each operation. The only operations ever performed in the maternity theatre are Caesarean (or more colloquially labelled 'C') sections. Our morning list consists of three 'elective' C-sections, the kind that are planned in advance, scheduled to meet the needs of the parents or unborn child, but to fit in with the surgeon's list. The women come into the ward, one of the other midwives runs through their paperwork and prep, and they await their theatre time. Routine, simple, straightforward. The only deviation from the plan tends to come when the theatre is needed for an urgent C-section, the unplanned kind; the women who need to have their babies delivered stat. Being unplanned, these can happen any time of the day – or night.

There's only one obstetric theatre at St Paul's so we can only have one case at a time. When I'm out working on the ward, I never think of the women as *cases*, but stuck in theatre, gowned up and sterile, separated from the person on the table by drapes that prevent me from seeing all but a square of abdomen through which the incision and delivery are performed, sometimes I skip into that medicalised jargon. It becomes impersonal, I'm distanced, one step removed from the woman. Sometimes I don't even see her face until the suturing has been completed and she's ready to be taken to the recovery area. What I do see is the inside of her belly, the warm red space where the baby is, and then, soon after, is not.

Today, sleep-deprived and thinking of other things, gazing into internal spaces is the last thing I want to do. That strand of hair dangles into my eyes. I fumble the retractor when the surgeon asks me to pass it, and barely grab it before it slips.

"Sorry," I mumble from behind my mask.

"Heavy night?" the doctor says.

"Not the kind of heavy you mean."

I raise my eyebrows behind the visor, and she nods her head in a demonstration of understanding.

The anaesthetist has chosen the music for today's list, so we have the background buzz of some classical tune that I don't know the name of. He gets to sit at the more pleasant end of the theatre table, on the side of the drapes where the woman is happily chatting away to him whilst the surgeon has her hands inside the uterus, scooping the fetus up and out, delivering the baby. She's telling him about her holidays the year before, as my colleague wraps the baby in a towel, the paediatrician looks it over and nods, and they present the perfect, bundle of a boy to his mother.

Delivery is the quick part. It's the suturing and stapling back together that take the time. I pass the suction, the sutures, the swabs, and receive them back from the doctor in a finely choreographed order.

I count every item, check off every instrument used. There's no time to think about anything else whilst I'm focussed on the procedure. It's a meditative process. As I count the swabs, the theatre assistant repeats the numbers, marking the total on the whiteboard. It's a chant, a duet between us. I slip deeper into the meditation. The warmth of the theatre and the rhythm of the count are soporific, and I start to feel myself keel like a floundering ship.

"Violet!" Dr Goldsmith calls out and then turns to the assistant. "Get her a stool"

I can sit while I'm scrubbed. The slit up the back of my gown allows my bottom to pop through the sterile field as I fall back onto the plasticised seat. I'm wearing scrubs, thankfully, I'm not exposed like one of the patients would be.

"You. Get one of the others to switch in. Take Violet through to recovery and give her some water."

The doctor snaps orders, and everyone runs to attend to them.

"I'll be okay," I say.

"I need to get Mrs…" The doctor flicks her eyes to the wall where the woman's name is written in dry-wipe marker on the board. "Davis sutured. I can't nurse you as well, Violet."

"Really. I'm sorry. I'm still sterile. I'll get back in. I was just hot."

Goldsmith pauses, casts a look over me, and I assume she is calculating in her head the time it would take to get someone else scrubbed up and ready to work, rather than risking me having another wobble.

"Okay. You," she points at the assistant. "Get a fan. On that side near scrub nurse." The assistant hurries off and I unfold myself from the seat, getting back to the action.

"I'm so sorry," I say again, but the doctor is already holding her hand out for the needle.

"Suture," she says blankly, and we continue.

I have lunch in the little cafeteria next to outpatients. Mainly because I like to get off the ward for a little while when I'm working, but also because I haven't brought any food with me today. After a quick, dull sandwich I head back to the ward, where I have another two hours to get through before I can escape. I feel fine following my *episode* earlier, especially once I have eaten. I tell myself that I was hot, tired, hungry, and that I definitely was not having an anxiety attack. I tell myself this firmly enough and repeatedly enough that I believe it. Who knows? I'm not the doctor.

I swig a can of diet cola and then I send Zoe a text message before heading back to put my bag into my locker.

Sorry about Adrian. He's a dick sometimes. Want to get coffee after work so we can talk shit about him? 4 at Coffee Express?

Neither of us have access to our phones during the working day. I'm here in the hospital, where my phone can interfere with the monitors and machinery, and Zoe is in a school, where using her phone would break the same rules that the kids are bound by. After texting her, I slip my phone into the pocket of my bag and stow it away until after my shift.

When I return to my locker, shift completed, tired and stressed, there's the message that I expected from Zoe, and the silence I expected from Adrian.

She's written:

Not your fault. Don't apologise for him. <3 see you at 4

Perfect. I have time to get home and shower. Wash away the working day, wake myself up, think about the future. Washing and waking up seem uncomplicated and welcome. Thinking about the future is just the opposite. I know what I need to do, but I'm not sure if I can do it. Can I really leave him?

In Coffee Express, I keep my eyes down, looking into my latte, but I know Zoe is staring at me. I can feel the tension between us, like the static in the air when a storm is about to begin. I inhale, starting to form a sentence, but before I can speak her hand is on my wrist. I instinctively jerk back and send the white porcelain mug flying to the floor.

"Jeez Violet."

She's as shocked as I am. Is this what it's come to? Flinching at the slightest movement towards me?

The waitress is making her way over, heading to assess the situation, survey the damage. I expect to see anger in her face, but it shows only the kind of resigned acceptance that comes from clearing up after clumsy customers for far too long.

"Sorry," I say, and the word comes out like a drip from a tap that's running dry.

She doesn't say anything, and just busies herself with sweeping the chunks of coffee cup into a dirty blue dustpan. Zoe waits for the woman to leave before she starts to talk again.

"If you were me...and I was you...what would you be saying to me? What would you do?"

I'd keep my opinions to myself. I'd realise that I couldn't even begin to understand what you're going through when my life is so fucking perfect. I'd let you make your own decisions and support you as a friend. I think these things, but even though my instinct is to snap defensively like a cornered cur, I stop myself. I take time to consider my response.

"If anyone treated you like that, I'd..." I want to say I'd kill him, or I'd rip his balls off or something similarly violent, but that's just not me. I wouldn't. I cower rather than counterattack; I protect myself and try to pacify. When I saw Adrian speaking to Zoe like he did, what did I do? Did I get up, stand up for her? Did I sit there impotently like an idiot? I know. I know what I did.

We did a conflict resolution course at work, after an irate husband went for one of the doctors. Stay calm, they told us. Don't get involved in a dispute. Keep calm. Get out of the situation as soon as you can.

"I'd tell you to get out. As soon as you can," I say. It's the correct response. I think it's the truth.

There's still a sharp triangle of ceramic on the floor, just by the leg of my chair. A white rectangular reflection from the strip light above glints off it, like the sparkle of a fairy light.

"Look at me, Violet. Look at me."

I do as Zoe asks me. She's crying. Right here in the middle of Coffee Express. Crying. It's that silent, controlled type of crying that you can get away with in places like this, but I can see the course of the tears down her cheeks, cutting through her make-up, leaving two bare channels through the foundation and blusher.

How can I do this to her? How can I make her go through this with me? My own face glows with the fire of shame and sorrow: a pitiful cocktail.

"Zoe please. Don't. I'm sorry."

And now I know this is the truth. Whatever else, I can't bear to see Zoe cry.

"I'm not crying for me; I'm crying for you. Because there's nothing I can do or say to make this better for you. Because you got stuck with that asshole, and he's so much of an asshole that he's somehow convinced you that you are the one who is the cause of all this. He's made you believe that you did something to deserve the way he's treating you. I'm crying because

I remember the Violet Cobham who existed before she was replaced with this sheepish girl who jumps when her best friend moves close to her, and smashes up Coffee Express."

She offers a tiny, hesitant smile, and wipes at her cheeks with a rough paper napkin, smearing mascara over the red lettering.

I return the smile as best as I can. I want to join her in tears, but I don't cry for myself. Not here anyway. It feels terribly self-indulgent to open the floodgates and let out all the emotion that's held behind the dam of my controlled exterior. Zoe can cry; she can show how she feels without appearing weak or hopeless or helpless. If I cry, I'm acknowledging that it's all I have left. I've never been comfortable being open with my emotions, and I don't want to start to feel comfortable about crying. I won't accept it.

"I shouldn't accept it," I say.

The truth is creeping up on me, slow and steady, like the tide sweeping into a bay, pushing me against the cliff face with nowhere to escape it. Closing in with its certainty.

I've turned into a walking, wincing cliché. I barely recognise this pathetic person that I have become, that he has created. Zoe and I have sat in this coffee shop so many times over so many years. We have seen it change from an independent café and bookstore to the Coffee Express franchise that it is today. It has seen me change from a confident teenager to a crushed twenty-five-year-old.

Okay, so he has never laid a finger on me. Do I think that he would? I don't think that he wouldn't. Abuse is not a competition. If I've suffered more, or less, or differently than someone else, does that make my experience any less significant? If it's his words that have worn me down rather than his fists, does that matter? He has done this to me. It's time for me to leave.

CHAPTER THREE

I get home at six, and by half past I'm deep into it with Adrian.

"It's no good. There's nothing you can do to make me change my mind. Not this time, Adrian. I'm sorry. It's over." I am resolute, but I am saying the words for myself as much as for him. I won't change my mind. I won't. I must convince myself by saying it out loud.

"No," he says, as if I haven't been clear enough. As if it is still up for debate. "No. You are not leaving me. No."

There's a snarling ferocity in his voice that sets me on edge. He's on his feet, moving towards me, and I know it's time that I should get out of here. I glance over my shoulder towards the door, towards my escape route, not wanting to take my eyes off him for too long. If I lose sight of him, I'm afraid that he will pounce.

"Adrian. I am going. Please. Look." I wave my car keys. "I'm just going to open the door now, go out to my car, and leave. I'll come back for my things when you are at work, I won't disturb you, I won't…"

"You won't leave me!"

He yells the words at me, and luckily, I am taken by surprise and flinch. Lucky because he picks up the mug of tea from on the counter beside him, and he flings it across the room, and it narrowly misses my head.

"Fucking hell, Adrian. What the absolute fuck?"

I don't know what else to say. He flies towards me. He's fired up, not thinking straight, out of control. What happens next comes all at once, like a slow-mo movie scene. I stand, immobilised, as he swings his fist back, and I watch it move towards me. I want to tell him to stop. I want to duck out of the way. I want to avoid what I know will be a painful impact. Instead panic grips me and I drop to the floor. I just about have time to think how thankful I am that I can't handle stress, and I have this hyped up anxiety response, as I slip. I hear the thud of his fist into the wall behind where my head would have been, before I pass out.

When I start to come around, Adrian is sitting with his back to the door, his legs bent at the knee, arms gripping them in a hug hold as he slowly rocks. He's muttering something to himself that I can't hear. He is gingerly stroking his right hand with his left in a weird, contorted embrace. He doesn't notice as I open one eye and then the other.

"Adrian," I say. "Adrian. What the fuck?" My vocabulary seems to have become limited by his violence. I always tried not to swear in front of him, to be more lady-like and polite. Now, I am letting loose.

I should probably be dragging myself to my feet and scrambling to the door, but he looks pathetic rather than predatory.

"Oh man, I can't believe I did that," he says. He shuffles over to me and reaches out to put an arm around me. I pull away.

"No," I say. "Don't"

He nods slightly.

He's still holding his hand, guarding it, cradling it in the hand that he didn't almost hit me with.

45

"Are you okay?" I ask. I must ask. I don't feel threatened, now. I do feel concern for Adrian though, as messed up as that might seem.

"I bust my hand. I can't believe I…I was going to hit you. I…I'm so sorry."

I believe him. He's never done anything like this before. Never once has he physically hurt me in any way. I believe that he is sorry. Regardless of whether I believe that or not, though, this is really, absolutely, definitely the end. Some things are so far across the line that if you turned around you wouldn't be able to see the line anymore. He thought about hitting me. If I hadn't had one of my panic attacks, I believe that he would have hit me. That is what I believe.

"It's done now," I say. "It's done. Look, I really am leaving now." I slowly pull myself to my feet, but he stays on the floor.

"I've messed up, haven't I?" he says. I nod.

"It's…not the best." I somehow manage a tiny smile, but the situation is beginning to feel quite surreal now. His hand looks purple-blue. It's mottled and unnatural.

"You're going to need to have that looked at." I nod towards it, and he looks down, wincing.

"It'll be fine. It just hurts a little."

"Really. You need to get it seen. It looks pretty bad."

He looks at the bruised mess again and nods his head.

"Would you take me, Violet? Please?"

I don't want to spend another moment in his company, but I can't bring myself to refuse him. It's not that I still care about him, it's about doing the right thing, being a decent human.

"Okay," I say. "But Adrian, I need to hear you say that you understand I am leaving."

He nods.

"Say it." I stand over him, my keys in my hand. "Please."

"For fuck sake, Vi. Okay. I get it."

I don't want to be stuck for four hours in accident and emergency with him. I couldn't bear it. I stick my keys into my pocket and pick his bunch off the counter.

"We'll take your car. I'll get Zoe to pick me up when we get there."

A plan forms in my head. I can come back, get my things while he waits to be seen in casualty. He has given me the perfect get out. Own goal, Adrian. Well done.

He opens his mouth to complain, but instead he sighs and throws his good hand into the air.

"Fine. Whatever. Just drive carefully."

I drive carefully, but I drive quickly. I want this done. I want it over.

I see Adrian into the sour lemon-lit waiting room of A&E and leave him sitting on the plastic seating. I walk away a few steps and then make the biblical error of looking over my shoulder. His head is dropped low between his legs, like someone trying to stave off a nosebleed. My first instinct is to run back to him, to tilt his head up, kiss him, make everything better. Nothing is going to be *better*, I tell myself. Still, I can't quite stop myself from heading back over. I can do one small thing before I message Zoe and ask her to pick me up.

"Hey. Do you want me to fetch you something from the machine?" I'm thinking of fetching him a cola or bar of chocolate, something to take his attention, as a substitute for me. My aim is to placate him, like a mother taking away a pacifier and handing over a new toy car instead. Adrian loves his sweet things, so I'll replace one with another. This thought makes me smile, and Adrian thinks the smile is for him; I let him.

"Thanks, hon. Just a cola."

He doesn't offer any money, but I guess as I suggested it, he assumes it's my treat. Why not? Old times sake and that. I don't let my smile drop until I walk away, and I don't take out my phone until I'm around the corner, out of eyeshot.

Zoe. I'm in A&E. Can you come? I'm sorry.

Almost instantly I see the little dots that mean she's typing a response, and then her reply pops up.

Are you ok? What has he done?

Of course, her instant reaction would be to assume that Adrian has hurt me. He has hurt me, but not physically. Before today I would have said that he's not that kind of man. Whatever else he is, he's not abusive. I check myself. He's not abusive in that way. He is abusive. Of course, he is. Abuse comes in so many flavours. The kind I saw between my mother and father, that gradual shutting down and exclusion, the distancing and the deceit. The kind I went through with the guy before Adrian, that even now I don't want to talk about. Some things you put into a burlap bag in the darkest reaches of your mind, put that bag into a chest, wrap it in chains until all you can see is a metal shell, and the memories that you've stored are so obscured that you can't even bring them to the surface if you try. You won't ever try.

I realise that I'm spacing out, and Zoe has frantically sent another message.

I'm setting off. What's happened?

The little dots flash up again and I quickly type a reply before she can send another message.

It's not me, it's Adrian. I'm fine. Will explain everything when you get here.

And then I add

Thanks Zoe xx

I put my money into the vending machine and select Adrian's cola and my bottle of water. They clunk into the bottom, and I reach my hand in to pick them out. His can is ice cold, tiny beads of condensation gathering into tiny tracks of tears. Something inside me snaps, and I toss his drink into the trash, taking only my drink back to the waiting room. I'm not in any hurry. I stop to read a poster about hand hygiene, suddenly enthralled by the joy of infection control. I see this poster every day at work, there's one on every ward, in every clinic, and I've never more than glanced at it before. Today, it's the most fascinating artwork that I've ever seen.

I open my bottle and take a slow deep drink of the water. I didn't realise how hot I was until I feel the chill cooling my throat. I realise I haven't eaten since lunch. I had my latte at Coffee Express, but that's all since my crappy sandwich at work. I check my purse for change and go back for a chocolate bar. Not the healthiest option, but it's a special occasion, so what the hell. I open it and eat it greedily in three bites, standing right there in front of the machine. It tastes like freedom.

Zoe is on her way, and when she arrives, I'm out of here. There's no reason for me to sit awkwardly with Adrian. I'm not going to comfort him, I have no chirpy conversation to make, all I have is resentment and bitterness.

I drink another slug of the water, to rinse the chocolate smell from my mouth, and head back to the waiting room.

"Sorry," I say. "Yours got stuck." I add a cute little shrug, to give the impression of being apologetic. "I didn't have change for another."

He looks at me, and I think he's about to say something when his name rings out over the tannoy.

Adrian Cooper to triage.

The first step of many in his wait to be treated. He stands, and looks down to me, expectantly. I make no move to join him, and I keep my face expressionless. You're on your own this time, buddy. You're on your own from now on.

CHAPTER FOUR

The next two weeks pass in a whirl of flat hunting. After viewing and rejecting five different options on my limited days off, I'm coming to the end of my list. Zoe and Luke have been the perfect hosts but squatting in their spare room is starting to feel like an imposition, even though I know that I'd do the same for her. I also know I'd never have to. Something about their complete, unfettered kindness makes me feel weak and vulnerable. I need to get out of here for my own good, not because they don't want me here. Zoe would let me live here forever if I wanted to.

I don't know what I expected from Adrian, but after a few unanswered texts on the first couple of days after I left, he gave up. Nearly two years together, and it was all over, just like that. A masochistic part of me wanted more from him. That part wanted him to send me countless messages, come over to Zoe and Luke's and try to drag me home. That part of me wanted to be pursued. There seemed something so very unfinished about the finality of me leaving, and him just letting me go.

Still, I turn my attention to looking for a new, permanent, home, and my thoughts of Adrian slowly fade to relief that I got away from him. I'm certainly not moping and wishing that things had been different. My biggest worry at the moment is that I'll have to settle for a room in a shared house. There are only two other flats that I've listed as *suitable*? and I'm crossing everything that the question mark is unnecessary. I needn't have worried. The next apartment that I visit is a small, unremarkable, but perfectly acceptable one-bedroom rental. There's a separate living room, and a cute but tiny kitchen. The bathroom has a bath, which you might think is a given, but the majority of flats that I've visited have only a shower cubicle, sink and toilet. They had me at *bath*. I go to see it after work on Tuesday afternoon, and fall in love. I fill in the paperwork, leave a holding deposit and by the end of the week I've moved out of Zoe's and into my own place.

It's weird at first, being on my own again. I've been used to Adrian's presence, whether I've liked it or not. It feels a little like I have a phantom limb. I'm aware of the absence of something, and that something still causes me pain even though it's no longer there. His aftertouch is an itch that I try to ignore. The pain is heavily offset by the simple pleasures of being able to eat when I want to, sleep when I want to, and, you know, generally being able to be happy without him crushing every fragment of joy from my life. I gradually start to feel happy, genuinely happy, about being single and independent.

I'm reflecting on this in the hospital cafeteria. After a standard, stressful morning on the ward, I'm glad to sit down, on my own, with lunch and my Kindle. I've found that since Adrian's enforced absence from my life I have a lot more time to do the things that I want to. I don't have to feel guilty any more for hogging the bathroom or being out of Adrian's company for too long, so I can now enjoy hot baths. I can pick up a book, or the electronic version, and read as much as I want to, as often as I want to. Before bed last night I had reached an exciting part in my current novel of choice, and I've been waiting all morning to click open the Kindle to see what happens to Eva and Mark.

"Is this seat free?"

A man is pushing his tray onto my table, not waiting to hear the response. My mouth is busy chewing a cheese sandwich, so I can't reply anyway. He sits, I look back down at my electronic book.

The large plastic tray cramps the space on the tiny circular table, and almost nudges my cup onto the floor.

"Sorry," he says, but he doesn't unload the tray or make any attempt to give me more room.

I'm not in the mood for conversation. I'm rarely in the mood for conversation on a good day, but the morning has been full of lost records, waiting for doctors to review patients for discharge and a general irritating backlog. My lunch break is meant to be at twelve, but the clock tells me it's twenty past and I've only been here for ten minutes. I finish at half past three, and if I wasn't so hungry, I'd have pushed through to the end of the day and knocked off early. I needed this break. Sometimes alone time is...

"What are you reading?"

He's craning his neck around to try to see the text on my Kindle, clutching his pastel blue hospital issue mug by its handle so precariously that I think its contents are almost certainly going to end up on my screen.

I read to the end of the sentence, and tell him it's the new Donna Smith, expecting him to give me a blank look, and hoping that it will end the conversation. I punctuate the end of my spoken sentence by looking back down to the e-book and continuing to read.

"She's great," he says. "I loved that one about the woman in the woods."

"Yeah," I say. I take another bite of my sandwich, read another line, try not to make eye contact.

"Sorry. You're trying to read and eat and I'm some silly stranger who turns up and interrupts you."

I think this means he is going to stop talking to me, but it turns out that I am wrong. Instead, he holds out his hand towards me, even though my sandwich is in one hand and my Kindle is in the other. I sigh in a way that I hope isn't too obvious, put my sandwich onto my plate and click my screen off.

"Matt," he says, as he shakes my hand.

He shows no sign that he's aware of how much he has disrupted my quiet lunch.

"Violet."

"Like the flower. How pretty. Was the flower named after the colour or the colour named after the flower?"

I don't care.

"I don't know," I say. I smile, because it's the polite thing to do, he smiles back, and then I smile for real. He's not bad looking.

Working in the maternity department, the only men I tend to encounter at work are either doctors or the partners of the patients. I don't have anything against doctors but there has never been one that I would like to date. Never say never I suppose, but probably never.

I stop myself before I get carried away. He could be the partner of one of the patients, but it's a big hospital and the cafeteria covers all the wards, so the odds are in my favour. I haven't stopped myself enough, clearly. I have the kind of imagination that does this. As soon as I meet someone, my mind cycles through scenarios, picturing different probabilities and possibilities. If I let myself, I could describe the first Christmas that we might spend together or tell you the name of the dog that we will choose together from the shelter, or, and this is what I am best at, I could speculate on how our relationship will end. Two minutes, Matt has spent in my company, and I'm already picturing our whole relationship and breakup. Luckily, he has no idea what is going on in my head. However, my hand has started to shake slightly, my cheeks have turned the same colour as my pale raspberry lipgloss, and my breathing rate has increased.

"Oranges," he says, and the spell is broken. The confusion cuts through my creativity.

"What?"

"I was thinking of oranges. The colour was named after the fruit, not the other way around."

I have no idea how to respond. I raise my eyebrows and tilt my head back slightly, quizzical and curious.

"Yeah, before the days of the fruit it was called...oh I can't even remember now. Yellow-red or something. Not very imaginative."

"And yet strangely accurate," I say, and smile again. So, this is small talk.

There's something hypnotic about him. I want him to keep talking. I want to pick up my sandwich again, and finish it while I still have time, but I'm suddenly self-conscious.

I have fifteen minutes more.

"You must work here," he says.

"Must I?" The words come out in a less friendly tone than I intend. "I do, yeah. I must. How did you guess?"

It's sarcasm. I'm dressed in my midwife's uniform, but still, he nods his head to the lanyard around my neck. My work badge is tucked inside my uniform during my break, but the hospital's branding is visible on the woven fabric that peeps from beneath the opening at my neckline. I look at his collar, no lanyard. So, he doesn't work here.

"No, I don't." He reads my mind, or at least reads the direction of my gaze. "I'm visiting my mother, actually."

My sandwich is raised halfway to my mouth, and I pause when he says this.

"Oh, she's fine," he says, gesturing for me to continue. "She's a doctor. I just had to drop something off for her."

The relief of not having to sympathise with a stranger about his sick relative is a rush. I relax, nod, and put the remains of my lunch into my mouth. Chewing gives me an excuse for not knowing what to say. He drinks some more of his tea and pretends not to look at me. In an awkward silence we sit like two mathematicians trying to solve a problem, both knowing that it's possible but that it might take them some time to get to the correct answer.

"I have to go back to work," I say. I have more time, but I'm trying to create a sense of urgency, as though my presence is a limited offer.

"Of course," he says. His eyes are a clear, pale blue, like the sky on a cold winter morning. I want to stare into them, I want to have the right to lose myself in them. Instead I steal short, punctuated glances.

There's a sense of there being more to be said between us, but neither of us know how to say whatever it is. I feel like I'm on a stage, the audience staring at me, waiting for me to recite the next line, while I stand, dazzled dumb by the spotlight.

Two months ago, I was living with Adrian, thinking that I could, possibly, maybe spend the rest of my life with him. Sometimes that was not a positive thought. Now, I'm sitting in a glass-walled cafeteria, half-thinking of this afternoon's clinic paperwork, and half-captivated by some tall, handsome stranger. Our conversation has been flat, and yet somehow, I know that there is something here. I'm a prospector, panning for gold. I saw the glint; I know it's there. I know it.

It's just one of those things though, isn't it? A missed connection. Two people, wrong place, wrong time. I'm not ready to date anyone now, I can't be. Adrian is still a fresh wound that hasn't scabbed over yet. A hot man sat at my table and spoke to me and I went a bit silly, that's all that's happened here.

"It was nice to meet you," I say, as I stand and push in my chair.

"Short, but sweet," he says, and flashes that smile again.

His lips are plump little pillows. Another scenario pushes its way into my mind, and I push it back down.

I pick up my Kindle, and head for the door. As I pass behind him, he reaches out his hand, almost making me trip in surprise as it collides with me.

"Hey!" I say, but it's surprise, not a protest.

"Here," he says. I look down and see he is passing me a small white card. His business card. His number. Matthew Chisholm. Architect. How professional it looks, how intriguing he is.

I nod, I smile, I put the card into my pocket, and then, I go back to work.

CHAPTER FIVE

I leave it a couple of days before I message Matt. I know that you're not supposed to contact someone straight away when they give you their number. It's a weird reverse-etiquette type rule, but I stick to it because I wouldn't want to look desperate. I'm actually more reluctant than desperate. I certainly wouldn't consider myself to be on the lookout for a relationship. My encounter with Matt was unscripted and unexpected. I'm still licking my wounds from the whole Adrian thing, and I'd kind of decided to have some alone time, some time to be by myself. To be myself.

I take the business card out of my purse and turn it over in my hand. Smooth off-white colouring, the text indented, forming an impression that I can trace with my finger, through the letters of his name. Matthew Chisholm. Architect.

Before I message him, I do what any normal millennial would do, and I check out his social media presence. It's surprisingly sparse. No Facebook, a LinkedIn profile that I don't even bother looking at, and nothing on the website for the company he's based at. All I know about him is that he is quite attractive in an Eddie Redmayne kind of way, all cheekbones and smile, but with rusty brown hair. I wish I could gather more intel, stalk him a little, but there's nothing else. Either he's a very private person or a very dull person. Let's find out.

Hi Matt. It's Violet. Thanks for your number.

I type and then delete. I'm the dull person, it seems.

Fancy another date in the hospital café sometime? Violet x

I debate deleting the kiss, but I reason to myself that it's normal, that everyone adds these things to their messages, and it doesn't necessarily mean that I'm going to kiss him. I want to kiss him. Of course, I do. It's near the top of my 'to do list'. If he wasn't so gorgeous and charming and funny, I would probably have thrown the card into the bin and moved on with my life, but he appears to be all of those things, and

66

even though I'm not sure that I'm ready for anything serious so soon after Adrian, I'm ready to text Matt and see where this goes.

The truth is, I've never really been on my own. I'm a self-professed serial monogamist. I flit from one relationship to the next, never really stopping to take a breath. I wanted it to be different this time. I thought leaving Adrian was the perfect time to take stock, to do some things alone, explore my options. I haven't ever travelled abroad, and I wouldn't want to be in a relationship and then leave on a journey of self-discovery. I want to go to yoga classes and book clubs. I want to go to gin festivals without it being seen as a crime. I want to not to have to answer to anyone. But who am I without a boyfriend? I hold my hands up. That's the most ridiculous non-feminist thing I've ever thought, but still, I do think it. I define myself by my relationships with others. In my work life, I'm a fierce advocate for women. I stand up for them, I fight for them, I do everything I can to promote their rights and independence. Personally though, I'm shackled by my own lack of self-worth and self-confidence.

Matt replies to my message a lot more quickly than I expected, and the shrill beep of my phone takes me by surprise.

Anywhere you want, Miss Violet. Sister Violet? Friday evening okay?

He doesn't add kisses to his text, and I'm worried that I was too forward. Then a second text pops up.

xx

Okay. Stop worrying so much, Violet. I like the way he typed "Miss Violet", there's something very sweet about the phrasing. I'm not quite Sister Violet yet. I'm still at entry level as a midwife, a junior, some way to go before I achieve sister status. The ward sisters have a lot more responsibility than the junior staff midwives. They make important decisions, manage the ward, and they are always on hand to give a second opinion or advice when more junior staff, like me, need it. Caring for a pregnant woman and her baby is a lot of responsibility in itself, of course. Maybe that's enough for me. Perhaps I'll never want to be a sister. I'm flattered that he has suggested it though, which I assume was what he intended by his comment. It's easy to read things into text messages, but I do always search for the subtext, and I'm aware of my own.

Great. I'm on early shift Saturday so can't stay out too late. Dinner would be good. xx

Being limited by my working hours is a real pain in the ass sometimes. I need to at least try to be fresh for my shift. A seven-thirty start is no fun on less than eight hours of sleep.

I realise I haven't suggested a venue, but he covers this in his response.

Okay Cinderella. La Tosca is my favourite. That's alright for you? xx

It's a small, independent and, importantly, reasonably-priced bistro just off the high street. I've never been there, but I have walked past and smelt the aromas of tomato, basil, oregano, and sizzling steaks. Dinner, at a restaurant, with an attractive man. How lucky I am.

Great

I type and then realise I started the last message in the same way.

Perfect. What time is good for you? xx

I put the pressure of decision making onto Matt. This is somewhat of a habit with me. I don't want to say the wrong thing or make the wrong decision, so I would rather let someone else choose for me. That way, I can never have chosen badly. On reflection, I should probably have had someone choose my past romantic partners, and then they might actually have been romantic rather than...well, rather than the arseholes they turned out to be.

Is eight too early? Don't want to have to wait too long to see you xx

70

A flutter of a flush comes to my cheeks. He certainly knows how to talk the talk.

Same. Eight at La Tosca then xx

No point being coy about it. I'm not one for playing games. It's much better to be direct, say what you feel, go with what you think. If I am going to do this, I am not holding back. I know exactly what Zoe would say right now, I can almost hear her…*It's too soon. Be careful*…but I have a good feeling about Matt. My gut tells me that I should allow myself to be happy. My gut also tells me that I love Italian food and that La Tosca will be wonderful, no matter how my date with Matt pans out, so it's a win-win situation.

CHAPTER SIX

I spend a lot longer getting ready for my date than I had planned to. Keep calm, keep casual, I repeatedly tell myself as I tie my hair up, and then unpin it, straighten it, fluff it up again. I apply mascara, eyeliner, bronzer and deep plum lipstick, and then wipe it off to replace it with a neutral pink. I switch from stilettos to spikey kitten heels to ballerina flats, swap a low-cut wrap dress with a floral pattern for a white silk blouse and leather (effect) skirt, and finally opt for a polka dot tea dress. I feel like I am trying on different personas as I switch between outfits and styles. At work, I know who I am. I have the enforced routine of either theatre scrubs or pink midwives' uniform. My shoes are always flat and practical, my hair is always pulled up, off my face. My personal style has been stripped away. Looking at my reflection in the full-length mirror that hangs on the back of the bathroom door, I appraise myself as I would a stranger. With Adrian, I would dress to meet his approval. I knew what kind of clothes he liked to see me in, and I played the role that he created for me. I wanted to be 'Violet, Adrian's girlfriend'.

When I met Matt, I had been wearing my work uniform, my hair scraped up into a tidy bun, my makeup minimal, just a touch of foundation to cover my flaws, and a splash of mascara to stop me from looking so mole-faced. Looking like that, he was still interested in talking to me. He still gave me his number. I reason that whatever I wear tonight he will see an improvement on the woman he met after a busy morning, before a stressful afternoon.

He's even more attractive than I remember, as I see him waiting outside the restaurant for me. He's at least six feet tall, with his brick-brown hair in a planned-messy style. He's wearing jeans and an Oxford shirt, which match the style I've gone for this evening perfectly. We are in tune, now let's find out if we are singing the same song.

He kisses me on the cheek without waiting for an invitation. No hesitation, just a confident peck. I can feel my cheeks start to fill with scarlet as we head into the restaurant together. I'm not used to the attention, but I like it.

"So, you've been a midwife for a long time?"

He forms his questions like statements, for me to refute or confirm.

"You like your job?"

"You live in Cranbourne?"

"You're ready to order?"

It's one of those quirks that could start off seeming charming, but over time might wear thin on me, like a T-shirt that I really like but end up ripping up and using as a rag.

Much as I can envisage a future before I start a relationship, I can also see all the tiny things that are potential negative issues.

"Not really," I say. "I trained at the hospital here and I've worked here for two more years since then. It's not long."

"How does someone with no children end up wanting to be a midwife?" He puts a piece of chicken into his mouth and then pauses, chews quickly and swallows to add, "you don't have children?"

"No. I don't. I planned on being a nurse but changed my mind. Not that I don't like sick people, but…I don't think I could be around illness and unhappiness every day."

I ordered pasta, and I swirl the fork around a string of tagliatelle as I think about my past decisions.

"What about you?" I say. "How does someone whose mother is a doctor end up being an architect?"

"I don't like illness either." He laughs, I laugh. We have something in common. "Actually, that's not it at all," he says. "Well, it is partly that, but that's not the full story. It feels a little soon to be telling you my life story, but…" He pauses, puts his cutlery down and looks at me. "My mother was very…absent…from my life. From my family. When I was growing up, I barely saw her. My father hardly saw her. They never explicitly told me why they split up, of course. Parents don't talk to their kids about that, do they? But I'm pretty sure that was the main reason. She was always working. Evenings. Weekends." He pushes his cutlery together.

"Sounds like you had a tough time. I'm sorry."

I know what shift work is like. I understand how difficult it can be to hold down a relationship, to make time for someone.

"Yeah," he says. "Your food's okay?"

I take the hint and don't pursue the subject further.

"It's great. Really good."

I keep eating, but Matt doesn't touch any more of his meal. Half a breast fillet lies uneaten next to a pile of creamy mash. I decide not to ask whether he's going to finish it.

"Have you been here before?" I swerve.

"This place? Yeah, a few times. It's reliable enough. You usually eat locally?"

I have to think about this. Where do I *usually* eat? At home. At Zoe's. Adrian wasn't one for romantic dates and dinners out.

"Yeah," I say, in my most non-committal tone.

I try to play it cool, answering Matt's questions and asking enough but not too much. By the time dessert is being cleared away, we are leaning in towards each other, laughing.

When the bill arrives, the waitress slides it towards Matt.

"I'll pay my share," I say, but he's having none of that.

"I wouldn't dream of letting you pay on the first date. Wait until we're married for that." There's a moment of silence, and then we burst into laughter again. Neither of us has been drinking alcohol, we don't have the boozy giggles, it's just a natural, light easiness.

"Deal," I say, and he hands the waitress his gold card. At least it's gold-coloured, I don't really know what that means.

I've parked around the corner from the restaurant, and he walks me to my car. We stand on the pavement, beneath a lamppost. It's like something out of a romantic movie, and I'm swept along in the moment. I was determined not to kiss him on our first date, but as I stand in the lemonade light, I feel the fizz of excitement.

He leans in.

"Can I see you again?" he whispers into my ear.

I was expecting his lips to reach mine, but he swerved to ask the question. I'm disoriented.

"Wh-what?" I say.

"I want to see you again," he says. "Please."

His face looks so sweet, his expression so innocent.

"Yes," I say. "Yes."

And then, he takes my face between his hands, holds me firmly, but gently, and kisses me. It's a firm, almost chaste kiss, but it feels electric.

"And that's enough for our first date, Violet." He breaks off and smiles.

"I'll text you," I say, as he turns to walk away.

"I'll text you first," he replies, without turning around.

He doesn't see the smile on my face as I open my car door, slide in the driver's seat and shuffle my bottom in a little seated happy dance.

I drive home distracted and, for the first time in a long time, happy. It's not just the happiness of the present moment, I actually feel something else mixed in with the pleasure of the evening well spent. I feel hope. My mind starts to skip ahead again, to future dates, to time alone together, our romance blossoming, as they say in the movies. I put sharply on the reins and tell myself 'woah'. Slow up now. It's only a few weeks since I left Adrian. I am barely settled into my new flat and my new life. I've only just gotten used to what side of the bed I like to sleep on, which breakfast cereal I prefer, what day I do the laundry when I am left to choose for myself. I can leave my clothes strewn over the back of a chair when I take them off at night, and if I chose to do so I could simply toss them onto the floor. I could cocoon myself up in my duvet from the moment I get home from one shift to the time that I have to get ready to head out to the next – give or take the odd toilet break and fridge raid. I can catch up with Zoe after work, and not worry about how long our coffee dates last. I don't have to fear getting home late and facing the passive aggressive posturing from Adrian. Zoe and I can go out for vodka, stay home for prosecco, do what the hell we want to. Luke is so open to letting Zoe have her own space, her own time, room to be herself. Perhaps Matt will be like that too. Surely I can be myself *and* be in a relationship, if that's what I choose?

This is the twenty-first century. Feminism, girl-power, equality – everything I read in Marie Claire and Cosmo tells me that I can have it all. Now, I just have to decide what it is that I want.

CHAPTER SEVEN

Matt was true to his word, and he had already messaged me before I arrived home. Short, but sweet.

Had a fantastic night. You're something special, Miss Violet xx

I had smiled at my phone, but headed to bed without responding. Early mornings and late nights are not a good combination for me, especially when they are followed by another early morning. Yesterday I was awake from the darkness of morning to the darkness of midnight, and today I'm up at half past six for work again.

There's another message waiting from me from Matt, as I lean over to switch my alarm to snooze.

Have a great day. Can't wait to see you again xx

I admire his eagerness. It might be off-putting for some women, but after being starved for affection for so long from Adrian, and the guy before Adrian, I'm so hungry for it now. I don't want to rush things, though, so I leave the messages unanswered for the time being and go about my usual morning routine. I'm not playing games by not leaping to reply to Matt's messages. I hate games. I want to be honest and upfront. I want to be genuine, and that's what I feel like I am doing by not replying straight away. I am genuinely busy, and I'll get around to messaging Matt when I finally sit down for my lunch break.

I'm expecting to be working in the operating theatre again today, but we only had one elective patient scheduled and she went into labour overnight. Her Caesarean had to be moved forward. Extra work for the night staff, but not necessarily less work for me, as I'm working on the antenatal ward instead. The ward is my current rotation, but I help out in theatre just as often as I am here. The unit has been so busy recently that sometimes needs must, and not all of the midwives are trained, comfortable and confident to work in the theatre. Knowing which instruments are which, what you can and cannot touch when you're scrubbed up, how to anticipate and respond to the surgeon's needs, and keeping track of equipment and swabs, it all takes additional training. I was an eager student midwife, wanting to know everything, so I learned how to scrub, and now I'm always on the list for working in theatre. I'm not complaining, it gives me some variation in the workday schedule.

Being on the ward makes me remember why I wanted to be a midwife in the first place. I wanted to help people. It sounds like a cliché, but the truth is that I really did want to 'make a difference' for women and their partners. I still believe that the kind of support and care that women and families receive during pregnancy and the peripartum period has a massive effect on not only their experience at that time but also the years after. I'm too early in my career to see the long-term effects I might have had on people, but I've seen women come back for their second, third, fourth babies and hug the midwife they remember from last time they were here. I've seen older women, grandparents of newborns, who praise the midwives on the postnatal ward when they visit, telling them how they delivered their daughter and now their daughter's daughter. There's a sense of a special bond between a woman, a family, and a midwife. The word *midwife* literally means 'with woman' and being with women in this intimate way is a privilege.

Today, the ward is not overly busy. It's never *quiet* but *not busy* is fine by me. Not because I want to sit in the office, eat biscuits, top up my caffeine levels and think about Matt, not at all.

When there are fewer patients for each midwife to care for, there is more time to spend with each woman. *Patients* is not quite the right word. The very word *patients* conjures images of someone sick or infirm, and pregnancy is definitely not a malady. Calling women *patients* can be seen as medicalising them but calling them *clients* or *customers* sometimes doesn't feel right either. When I say *patient,* I don't mean it in a derogatory way. It's shorthand, and I don't always feel the need to politicise every word I say.

At handover, I am allocated three women to care for in a small four-bedded bay. Because I've mostly been working in theatre for my last few shifts, I've not met the ladies before. There's Heather, who thought she might be in labour, and has had babies with very quick deliveries before, so she's staying with us to be on the safe side, rather than risk giving birth in the kitchen or on the dual carriageway. Everything seems calm at the moment. Next to her, chatting away constantly about how excited she is about her forthcoming induction, is Anita. She's eighteen, confident and chirpy. If it wasn't quarter to eight in the morning, I would be much more willing to enter into conversation. I'll be back with her when I've had coffee and done the drugs round. I'm already looking forward to getting to know her. The final lady is Sofia, who is sleeping, or at least trying to. It's difficult, sometimes, to fit around the sleep-wake patterns of the other patients on the ward, and Sofia, like me, seems to prefer her mornings in bed asleep rather than awake and chatting. I don't need to disturb her yet, she is here so that we can monitor her blood pressure and the levels of protein in her urine, and she's not due for another set of observations for another two hours. All good. I introduce myself to Heather and Anita, and while they have breakfast, I grab coffee and sit in the office, read through their notes, and gossip with the other staff about my date.

I check my phone at lunchtime, meaning to reply to Matt, to find that he has sent me another two messages while I've been working. I obviously didn't explain to him clearly enough that I can't use my phone on the ward, but as his mother works in the hospital, perhaps I assumed that he already knew this. Assume. Makes an ass out of you. He's not an ass though, he seems very sweet, and from the fact that he has now sent me four messages to which I have not replied, he also seems *very* keen.

Are you busy tomorrow night? xx

Can't stop thinking about you. You're so gorgeous xx

Okay, over-keen perhaps. It is flattering though. Gorgeous? Am I? Not really. I'm a very average looking woman. I use the word *average* in a 'be kind to yourself' way that I have learnt from years of reading self-help and confidence-building books. I had Adrian, and the guy before Adrian, crushing my self-esteem, making me

86

feel like everything I did was wrong, or not good enough. To feel that I am even *average* is several steps up the ladder from where I was in the past. I stare at the word on my phone: gorgeous. When was the last time that anyone ever said that to me? Zoe tells me all the time. We go clothes shopping, taking our jumble piles into the changing rooms, switching from one outfit to the next. Off hangers, onto our imperfect bodies, parade in front of the mirror, look over the shoulder, check out the angles. What do you think? You look gorgeous. It's too small, too tight, too bright. Yes, you're probably right. Try the next. Every time though, no matter how I look, I am gorgeous, she is gorgeous. I love that girl.

Thanks.

I type that word because it seems like the right thing to say. And then

I'm on a late shift tomorrow. How about Wednesday? xx

When I add the kisses to the message this time, I mean every pointed, crossed line. The memory of his lips on mine, that fast, firm first kiss, is like a flash of lightning in my mind. It was a taster, and I want more. More kisses, that is. I stutter slightly at the thought of sex. In a prudish, pathetic way, I feel like I am not ready for a sexual relationship yet. Things change between two people when they take off their clothes and surrender to intimacy. A barrier breaks down between them, and things are never the same after that. I want the innocence of anticipation. I want to get to know who Matt is, and how we can please each other in other ways, which may be more intimate than sexual intimacy ever could be. Being naked in front of Zoe and feeling gorgeous is very different from being naked in front of a man.

Idiot, I think to myself. Too many romantic novels and slushy movies. In my mind I have this picture, an image of what life should be like. I have a romanticised vision of romance. After the relationships that I have had before, why shouldn't I strive for something better? Why shouldn't I want something perfect? If Matt is not the one to give me that, I don't have to settle. I don't have to be in a relationship at all. Perhaps I *am* being free. Perhaps I am being myself, making my own decisions now.

I'm sitting in the cafeteria, smiling to myself like a medieval fool, holding my phone and drifting in a sea of idealised thoughts. Just as I am about to bring myself back to reality and check the time, my phone buzzes in my hand and I jump with surprise, dragged from my dream state.

Perfect. Want to come over to my place? I'll make you dinner xx

Is it too soon? What assumptions will he make if I agree to go to his house, flat, wherever he lives? Assume, assume, assume. The question makes my head pound and my heart start to dance in double time. I feel my breathing skip out of rhythm, and have to get a hold of myself to calm my body functions before the panic sets in. Calm, Violet. Calm. I still have some water in the paper cup on the table in front of me. I sip at the ice-cold drink, then press the cool vessel to my forehead. Calm now. Calm. If thinking about going to

Matt's place makes me feel this way, then I already have my answer. It is too soon.

How about we go out somewhere instead? xx

As soon as I send the message, I wonder what assumptions he will make about my response. There it is again. Assume. Sometimes when you don't have all the facts to go on, when all you have are your past experiences and your best judgement, assume is all you can do. If he misjudges me for my desire to take things slowly and sensibly, is he really the kind of person I want to date?

Of course. Any excuse to go to a lovely restaurant with a lovely girl. You choose where. xx

Girl. There is that word again too. Seems I'm haunted by semantics today. You girls. Something bristles inside me as I read it and I tell myself, swiftly, to calm down. Don't overreact. Don't assume. I can feel the bubbling anxiety, the slow simmer rising. Too soon. Maybe it is too soon.

CHAPTER EIGHT

By the time I've worked through my late shift on Sunday and my early the next day, I'm exhausted and desperately in need of Monday's coffee date with Zoe. Typically, it's raining, and I get soaked between the tiny car park that I'm lucky enough to squeeze into, and Coffee Express just down the road. My dark hair is flattened in spiky points, forming fingers down my forehead. Zoe must have been here a little while because her red curls are frizzy-damp but not dripping wet.

Despite the balls of rain on my jacket, she embraces me and plants a firm kiss on my soggy cheek. The aroma of freshly brewed coffee mingles with her rose-scented perfume, and it soothes me somehow; it smells like home in a way that my new apartment doesn't quite manage to yet. These are my creature comforts: coffee and Zoe.

I put my cup onto the table and slump into the sofa. I asked for an extra shot of espresso today, but I'm not sure even that is going to be enough.

"That bad?" she asks, and I nod.

"Just long days. Late shift – early shift combos kill me. Still. I don't think I'll ever get used to them."

I'm not a morning person. Never have been. Even getting up at six am would be bad enough without having to work until ten the night before. The switch between lates and earlies wipes me out. I blow onto the foam on my latte, trying to cool it so that I can gulp it down.

"What's new?"

Zoe leans back, relaxing into the slouchy purple velvet chair.

"I…" I begin the sentence, and then change my mind. "Not much. Nothing really."

Too soon to be in a relationship. Too soon into dating Matt to tell Zoe about him. Like there's some kind of a timetable for these things. I flick my eyes up at her, over my cup, looking for a read. If she suspects anything untoward, she's not saying. She sips at her mocha and sighs.

"Did you ever imagine our lives would be this exciting?" She smiles. "I feel like we spent all our teenage years longing to grow up, to be older, to have independence and money to do things…"

"And, now we can do whatever we want to, we work every hour to earn money to live so that we can work every hour," I say.

"Paying for cars, so we can get to work, to earn the money we need, to pay for the cars. Saving up for holidays we can never have, because we are always too busy working to take them." She swirls her mug, as if about to read my fortune in the chocolate powder and coffee grains at the bottom.

"Ugh. Too relatable. Stop."

We both laugh, but my mind is flicking through the words we have said. We went seamlessly from wishing our youth away to working our twenties away, and I'm still holding back, slowing myself down, stopping myself from diving in and enjoying life.

My phone vibrates in my pocket, and I ignore it, but I hope that it's Matt.

By the time I get home and check my messages, there are three separate texts from him.

Hope you're having a good time with your friend xx

Message me when you get home. I miss you xx

Thinking about you, gorgeous girl. Hope you haven't forgotten me xx

They aren't really invitations to a conversation, they read more like observations and idle compliments. Face-to-face our conversation was effervescent. By text message it's falling flat. Perhaps that's my fault. I've never been one for holding long conversations this way. Sometimes there's gossiping with Zoe, infrequently I message some of the girls from work, but I never engage in a full-on discussion. I can't be bothered with Snapchat or group messaging. Give me good old face-to-face contact anytime, but not too much of it, thank you; I'm still an introvert.

Matt is trying to make contact in the only way he can. He's trying to build something between us. How can I feel anything other than flattered by this?

Had fun thanks. So how about Golden Gate on Wednesday? Eight o'clock again? xx

I'm straight to the point, trying to avoid the small talk.

What did you get up to? Did you tell her all about our date? xx

No mention of my suggestion. Okay. Is it weird for him to ask me whether I told Zoe or is he just making conversation? I need some kind of translation service to work out what lies between the words on a screen and the thoughts in Matt's head.

Drank coffee and laughed a lot. Didn't talk about you, but thought about you xx

True, fair, and enough information.

I put my phone down on the table in my little hallway, next to my keys and my purse. I'm one of those people that loses *everything* if they don't put them

96

in the same place every day. If I have one thing to thank Adrian for, its teaching me to leave my important items on this table, so that I always know where they are. Also, if I ever have to evacuate quickly, I can just grab them on the way out. My keyring with its inspirational message of "Seize the Day!" dangles onto my phone screen.

I don't have to work until two thirty tomorrow afternoon, so I've planned a night of mini-luxuries. When you've lived with someone, even time alone can feel like a luxury. I turn on the oven and stick in the leftovers of a pot of chilli I made yesterday morning. While it reheats, I run myself a bath.

I throw off my clothes and get into the tub, dipping my toe to check the temperature, and then sliding in, letting the foamy water swirl around me like amniotic fluid. I am safe, I am warm, I am relaxed. I close my eyes, listen to the silence, appreciating the moment, until my mindfulness is infiltrated as I hear my phone vibrate against my keys in a chiming brrr. I sink my head under the water, beneath the bubbles, letting them envelope me in warm silence. Tonight, it's just my night. Seize the night. Carpe bath time.

CHAPTER NINE

My feelings in the period between arranging to go on the second date with Matt and the advent of the date itself swing from euphoric to sensible to tentative, and back to euphoric again. By the time I head out to meet him at The Golden Gate on Wednesday, I have resigned myself to accepting the date for what it is, trying not to overthink too much, and taking things as they come.

The Golden Gate is a Cantonese restaurant not far from the town centre, not far from my flat. It's close enough to me for Deliveroo to not be an option, because even though it's the best takeaway in town I would feel far too guilty ordering from there and having the delivery guy bringing my food down the two streets to my home. I didn't suggest the restaurant with any intention to invite Matt home, but also, I didn't *not* think about that option. I have to be up early in the morning, so a night of wild abandon is probably off the table, but a few minutes of something, on the table or wherever is a possibility. I don't go for the rules of dating that say you have to wait for the third date to get naked. If I feel like it, and he feels like it, then there's no time limit. Just because I didn't want to go over to his place this early doesn't mean that I don't want anything. Dating in the twenty-first century is complex.

Matt offered to pick me up, not knowing quite how close to The Golden Gate I live. We are meeting at eight and it's ten minutes before. I'm still getting dressed. Simple make up, simple dress. Casual and cool. He won't notice that I'm wearing my nicest underwear unless we end up back here in three hours' time, but still, I'm ready for all eventualities. I reach for my grapefruit cologne but the slight scent of it coming from the bottle as I bring it toward me spins me into a flashback to that night at Zoe's. It makes me dizzy with nausea and I put it to the back of the spill of bottles on my dresser. Instead, I pick up a rose-scented perfume and spritz myself. That fragrance. That feeling of security.

When I arrive at the restaurant, Matt is standing outside, reading the menu through the window. I sidle up to him, stealthily. His face, bathed in a blue glow from the neon restaurant sign, looks cold and alien, and I stop sharply.

"Oh hi," he says as he sees me.

"Hi. See anything you like?" I think he's going to say 'you', but he doesn't bite.

"Noodles. Singapore noodles. I think. What's good?"

"Shall we go in and look properly?" I say, more to get inside and sit down, be warm, than anything else.

"Sure." He starts to lead me in, then pauses, turns and looks at me. "I should have said. You look wonderful." His smile is so warm and open, that I feel the kind of melting sensation that I thought was only found in movies and books.

"Thanks." My voice is quiet and tiny. I'm dwarfed by his confidence.

He leans and I think he's going to kiss me but instead he ruffles my hair, and I feel even smaller.

"Let's go," he says.

We order a huge amount of food and eat about half of it. Sweet and sour, noodles, pork in black bean sauce, chilli beef, rice, and spring rolls that melt in my mouth like small parcels of pleasure. I have a glass of cold white wine, and he has a couple of beers, but it's not a boozy evening. The conversation flows more freely than the alcohol.

We talk about what we have in common. Neither of us have brothers or sisters. Our sets of parents are divorced. We both identify as introverts, although I have my doubts that he is quite as reserved as I am, due to the many text messages he has sent me since we first met. He's assertive and maybe a little cocky. I like it.

We talk about our differences. He likes reggae and I hate it, but we agree that he won't make me listen to it and I won't mention my dislike again. We both enjoy eating, but I could have guessed that from the way we are devouring our meal.

"I like a girl who likes her food," he says. "Too many of you are hung up on staying stick thin, making the right impression on Instagram, fitting into an image."

"Mmrph," I nod in agreement, as I eat another sweet and sour chicken ball. I'm always a little uncertain how to respond when men say this. Is he calling me fat and saying it doesn't matter, or is he giving me free rein to eat what I want? If it's the latter, I didn't need the permission, but I welcome his support. If it's the first, well, I'm a bit on the curvy side but whatever. We are both here. I'm not hung up on it.

He has the slim kind of physique that looks like it comes from good genes rather than an active gym membership. He's packing away the noodles, just like I am, and I find myself imagining what he looks like underneath his clothes. Not in a sexual way, not yet, just the soft little curve of his belly. The red-brown fuzz of hair I expect to find on his chest and between his naval and…I stop myself before I let my mind wander too far.

We talk about movies we like and agree to make time to go and see a new mystery that I know Zoe wouldn't want to see with me. We like a lot of the same music, apart from the reggae, and chat in depth about the local gigs we've both been at, at the same time as each other, unknowingly in each other's presence many times before we finally met. All the coincidences, all the similarities, they conspire to convince me that this could be something special. That and the fact that Matt appears to be a decent, caring, witty, charming and downright gorgeous man.

At the end of the night, we stand outside on the pavement, neither of us wanting to be the first to break away, to say goodnight.

"So, when can I see you again?" he asks, gently running his hand along my arm.

I try to recall my off-duty, and frown as I visualise the blocks of time, fenced off, untouchable.

I'm on an early tomorrow but tomorrow is too soon. Late on Friday so that's a no go. I'm going out with Zoe on Saturday and then I'm back to late shift on Sunday. Monday is coffee with Zoe and chill before my early on Tuesday.

So…

"Wednesday?"

"It's Wednesday now," he laughs.

I smile back.

"*Next* Wednesday."

I swear he almost pouts like a toddler.

"But I want to see you before then. I don't think I can wait a whole week to be with you."

"I'm afraid you'll have to," I say.

His hand has stopped stroking my arm and has settled, just below the crook of my elbow. It feels a little uncomfortable and I withdraw.

"I'm sorry. I want to see you too," I say, like I need to give some reassurance. I run through the events of the week that are preventing me from being with him. When I tell him that I want to relax on my own on Tuesday evening I have a pang that feels something like guilt. I've been on two dates with this man. I'm not sure I should be feeling like this.

"We could meet after you finish work? Just for a couple of hours?" he says, and the pang stabs me again.

I sigh inwardly. I know how I feel at the end of a shift. After an early morning and a long day on my feet I'm never feeling at my most romantic.

"It's only one more day until Wednesday after that. Let's meet up then and have a good night." I want to make the compromise seem worthwhile. "You can come over to mine and I'll make dinner."

This seems to placate him, as he gives me a broad smile.

"Well, if you put it like that," he purrs. "Wednesday it is."

I smile back, but inside I tremble. He stills me with a gentle, tender kiss.

He doesn't lurch at me, sticking his tongue into my mouth like a hungry anteater into an anthill. Rather his lips form a soft double arch that invites me in. I feel an actual rush as we embrace and I'm blushing as I step backward.

"I can't wait," I say. There's no playing it cool. I'm hooked.

CHAPTER TEN

Saturday afternoon is a rare chance for a girlie shopping trip with Zoe. Her weekends are usually spent with Luke, but today he is elsewhere and as I'm finally finding a day off on a weekend, we have plans. I don't mind working Saturdays and Sundays. It's extra money, and I don't have kids to think about like a lot of the other midwives that I work with. Even when I was with Adrian, I wasn't that bothered about having weekends off. We saw each other enough, living together. We probably saw each other too much.

I've had my usual lie in and a hefty breakfast of eggy bread, washed down with two mugs of tea. I'm dressed casual-comfy style and I'm feeling like everything is good in the world. As I leave the house to meet Zoe, my phone gives me its happy beeping sound.

Have a great day with Zoe. Thinking about your gorgeous face xx

I grin and practically bounce out of the door.

I decide to walk into the town centre. It's about fifteen minutes by foot, but it's one of those crisp autumn days where being outdoors is a pleasure. Not quite the cold chill of winter, but the bright sun of summer has faded to a hazy pale shimmer. The town centre can be packed during August, the tourists like tiny ants pushing past each other up the high street as they gather souvenirs and gifts to take home with them from the special shops that pop up around June and are cleaned out and boarded up each year by September. There are empty windows speckled along the main thoroughfare now, where the temporary postcard and memorabilia shops took over from closed down traditionals like British Home Stores, Woolworths and Beechers. There aren't many places left to browse around, and I don't get the same buzz from shopping online as I do from meeting up with my best friend and chatting as we hover over a new dress that one or the other of us spots on a rack, leaves for half an hour as we circulate around the store picking up T-shirts and sweaters, and then comes back to, tries on and buys. Online I'm more likely to know what I'm looking for before I even head to a site. I suppose it stops me from impulse buying quite as often, but where's the fun in that? I love my impulses. I feed them regularly.

The other thing about shopping online is that – even though you can make yourself a coffee in the comfort of your own home while you browse – it's not exactly a social event. In between popping into department stores and cute boutiques, my favourite part of these girlie shopping trips is sitting with Zoe over a hot foamy latte and having some me-time with her. Us-time. We have our regular catch ups on Monday, but these hard-to-come-by Saturday trips out into town feel somehow more special. They are like a bonus.

I swing my legs through the leaves in the park, childlike, unrestrained. Despite the recent rain, the leaves are dry and crunchy now, a pile of reds and browns that practically demand to be kicked. They float in the air like falling feathers after a pillow fight. Children are dressed in their winter clothes already, the black, fake fur trimmed hoods, duffle coats, home-knitted hats and woollen gloves. Everything looks cosy. It's my favourite time of the year.

By the time I get to Coffee Express, I feel elated. Everything is finally going my way.

I order a Pumpkin Spice latte with a song in my voice, and then sit, breathing in its aroma as I wait for Zoe to arrive.

I'm a few minutes early, so I click open my phone and send Matt a message.

You're too sweet to me! Thank you. I'm thinking about you too. xx

At the moment I am, and I feel the tingling excitement as I let my mind wander over the memories of our dates, and the possibilities in our future. I try to rein in my over-active imagination and settle for contemplating what might happen when he comes over to my place. Was it too soon to ask him? It felt right. I love my impulses.

Before I can start to daydream too deeply, Zoe arrives, and reaches to hug me.

"Hi!" I say, and it comes out like a shrill little chirp.

110

"Hey. Hope you haven't been here long." She looks into my mug and sees that it's almost untouched. "Not too long then?"

"No, no. I was a tiny bit early, it's fine!"

My voice is still abnormally squeaky. Perhaps I have been used to the droll tones of unhappiness and this birdlike voice is actually how I sound when I'm not miserable. It's been so long that it's difficult to remember.

"You okay?" she says.

Perhaps I'm smiling slightly more than I have been lately, or perhaps she recognises my trilling too. I wasn't sure whether to tell Zoe about Matt yet, but it seems like I can't conceal it. My mood is transparent.

"Hmm, fine. Work has been stressful. But otherwise, everything else is good." I try to keep my tone under control, but I know I am failing.

"Everything else?"

She should have been a detective, rather than a teacher, although perhaps she uses this skill set well with the students if they start to step out of line or try to deceive her.

I breathe in and am about to make up a white lie or at least delay telling her about Matt for now, slyly omit the truth, but instead I find my tongue running away with itself and I start to spill the details. I tell her all about him.

"And so, we've seen each other a couple of times and…" I finish with a little shrug that means I have no idea what I'm doing.

The details have spilled rapidly, and I stop to take a sip of sweet, spicy coffee while I let Zoe digest them.

"Gosh," she says.

There's a short silence between us, while I drink and try not to make eye contact, and Zoe swirls her spoon around in her frothy foam.

"Are you not happy for me?" My voice is a squeak now, rather than a chirp.

"I just think maybe it's a little soon," she says. I love her honesty, but I'm not sure that I want to hear it. I don't want to think of anything in a negative way right now.

"Things happen when they happen. What am I supposed to do? Live like a nun until this randomly allocated period of...what? Mourning? Am I meant to be mourning my shitty relationship?"

"I was thinking more of 'healing'. You've had a really tough time and I think it might be better for you if you had a bit of time on your own, have fun for a little while, do some things for you."

Her voice is soothing and placatory; her smile is tender. Still, my hackles are raised. The atmosphere between us has shifted.

"Being with Matt *is* doing something for myself. I *am* having fun."

"You know what I mean. When was the last time you were single? You skip from one relationship to the next without taking time to breathe and reflect. It can be good to take a break."

"I didn't know you were keeping track of my dating history," I say, but I know everything about hers, and I know that my words aren't true. "I like Matt and I want to spend time with him. I can't believe you are being like this."

She opens her mouth, about to speak, but says nothing, and closes it again.

"What?" I ask. "Come on. If you have something to say..."

"Violet, chill. If you think you're ready to move on, fine. I'm here for you. I support whatever you decide, Okay? I'm sorry. I don't want to argue."

My mind is still catching on the words that she didn't say. It's as though I snagged my belt loop on the door handle and it's tugging at me, stopping me from moving on. This time though it's my turn to bite back my words.

"Okay. I'm sorry too."

I raise my right hand, and she high fives me. We are cool.

"Actually, I need to talk to you about something." She pauses, and then adds, "Someone."

"Someone?" I echo the word back to her, trying it out to see what it means.

"I guess it's your turn to judge me," she says. "Vi, I've met someone."

The words still don't make sense. She is with Luke. She has the most perfect, blessed relationship with a man who adores her. The question I want to ask is "What about Luke", but that's not what I say.

114

"How could you do that?" The words jump out of my mouth before I can swallow them back. Their tone is acrid; I hate how they feel in my mouth.

"After everything we just said, Vi? Really?" She wears the same expression as a child who has just been slapped. Surprise, hurt, shock.

"I just mean...how does that happen? How did it happen? Who is he? What's going on?"

She settles back into her seat, her shoulders drop.

"It sounds so clichéd but it's someone from work. And again, it sounds clichéd, but I didn't mean for it to happen. Maybe that's what affairs are, clumsy clichés."

"What they are is *wrong*," I say. "Are you not happy with Luke? You've never said that he is anything but wonderful. We are always talking about all of my issues and you have never once said that you're having problems."

I feel a fishbone of doubt tickling my conscience, like it's got caught up there and I have to pluck it out. Have I been so preoccupied with myself and my own issues that I haven't given her the opportunity to speak?

"No. I mean yes, I'm happy. I've not had anything to complain about. He is just as you say: wonderful. I suppose that makes what I am doing even more terrible. It makes me more terrible."

I don't know what to say. If she was in the kind of relationship with Luke that I used to have with Adrian, or with the guy before Adrian, or the guy before that...if she was suffering and unhappy, maybe I would be able to understand. Maybe I would be feeling compassion instead of confusion.

"I wanted to tell you sooner, but..." She pauses again digging around in her mind for the right words. "Well, to be honest, I'm ashamed. I genuinely do feel like it's a terrible thing. But like you said, things happen when they happen."

"Don't you use my words like that. Don't. It's nothing like the same thing. Zoe, this isn't like you. You're not that person."

"It turns out that I am." She looks away, not able to look at me any longer. Her face is tomato red, so flushed that I can barely make out her freckles anymore.

She fiddles with her cup, running her finger over the handle, tracing it like a rosary bead.

I want to know more but I don't want to know more. I'm curious but conflicted.

She speaks, still not making eye contact.

"I hate who I've become. Sneaking around, lying." It shows in her face, a look of disgust breaks through her blush. "Lying to Luke. I never thought I'd do that."

"How long has it been going on? I guess you've been lying to me too."

"Well, not lying. Not lying to you. Omitting to tell you the truth, sure, but not lying to you."

The word keeps spinning around us: lying. It's dominating the conversation. The room is spinning with the word, and there's a strange fizzy feeling floating in my head.

"Violet? Vi?"

My heart thunder-pounds I hear the galloping in my ears, and yet my body feels empty of blood as I drop to the floor.

"Violet! Someone. Please." They are the last words I hear as I sink into darkness.

There's a man standing over me, his face too close to mine, so close that I can smell the egg mayonnaise he was eating before he rushed over to help me. I'm sitting semi-slumped, my stomach squashed, and a throbbing pain coming from my left leg. I must have whacked it somehow as I fell.

"She's back," the man says. He puts his hand onto the table and pulls himself upright. I'm grateful for the space and take a deep breath of eggless air.

"What happened?" I say. My voice is tiny. It doesn't sound like it belongs to me.

"You just went," Zoe says. "One minute you were sitting there, fine. The next you were on the floor."

"Panic attack. Shit. It crept up on me."

Zoe helps me to my feet and then onto my chair. The man sets a glass of iced water on the table in front of me and I take a deep gulp. The storm begins to calm.

"You still have those?" Zoe asks. I've had more than I've told her about. I suppose we both omit the truth sometimes.

"Not often," I lie. I take another sip of water so that I don't have to say anything else and hope we can change the subject.

"All okay?" the man says. Zoe nods and he backs off.

"Eggy," I say.

"So eggy." Zoe smiles and puts her hand on my brow. "That feels better. Are you really okay?"

"Yeah," I lie again. "I got a bit hot, then it makes me all claustrophobic and…you know what happens."

"I thought they were a thing of the past."

I shift in my chair, pick up the glass again, but it's empty. I don't have a prop, there's nothing to distract me or divert my attention.

"Yeah," I say. "Anyway. I don't remember what we were talking about?"

"Ugh," Zoe says. "Nothing much."

"I remember enough to know that you're avoiding the subject now. I'm not going to hide the fact that I don't like what you're doing, but...if you can accept my decisions then I accept yours. Do you want to talk about it?"

She leans across the empty cups and hugs me awkwardly. This is us. This is our friendship. This is what we do.

CHAPTER ELEVEN

Zoe didn't want to tell me anything else about Theo. Not yet. Wait and see what happens. I feel much the same about Matt, so I accept it, and move on. After we have finished our coffee, I am sufficiently recovered to head on to the shops as planned. If there's ever a sign that someone is over a panic attack, it's that they can elbow their way through the Next sale, and come out the other side with two perfectly-fitting dresses, and a pair of flat ballerina pumps that they don't need, but just *have to have.*

Zoe keeps asking how I am, but she's seen my wobbles before and her concern is limited by experience.

"Honestly," I say, "I'm fine now."

She gives me a look, as if assessing me, checking if I am being honest as much as checking if I am actually as *fine* as I claim.

"Okay," she nods. "Where are we heading?"

I point over to *La Boutique,* a sweet little independent lingerie shop.

"I might need some new…things…" I say.

"New man, new things, eh?" Zoe laughs.

"Do you need any new…things?" I ask the question tentatively, I still don't want to discuss what she is doing with someone who is not Luke.

Zoe shakes her head.

"Much as I like the idea of buying some sexy new underwear, I think that Luke would be rather suspicious. I have worn the same black bra and pants combinations since…well, since I met him, to be honest. Classic black never goes out of fashion, does it?"

She's correct on both counts.

There's that implied link, between buying the underwear and the person who is going to see you in it. As a single woman, I have still purchased reasonably nice lingerie sets, I'm not one for plain cotton and big knickers. This is partially because I have to wear a uniform every day to work, and I don't have any choice in what clothes I have on the outside, so my underwear is all that I have the option to choose. I like bright colours, the kind of things that perhaps people wouldn't expect the professional, polite midwife to be wearing.

When I was with Adrian, I chose the kind of panties and bras that I knew he liked. Black, always black, and soft, smooth, silky. Now, I can decide what to wear, how to wrap myself for Matt. The feminist in me wrinkles her nose at the idea that I should have to do anything to change or present myself differently for a man, but part of it is for myself, for my confidence, to feel feminine and desirable. Make of it what you will, I'm not making a political statement, I'm just thinking about getting laid.

One of the aspects of Zoe's style that I admire is that she never caves in and follows the fashion. She knows what she likes, and she sticks with it. Everything she wears looks well-put together and thought out, but really, I know that she has a collection of items that just work for her, so no thought is needed. I envy that. Some days I look as though I have had a fight with a jumble sale and lost. Wearing a uniform every day isn't such a bad thing for me.

We head into *La Boutique* with its sparsely populated rails and racks, and I pull out a few items, holding them up for Zoe's approval as I do so. There's a yellow satin bra with triangular cups, that looks a little like a bikini. It feels rich, smooth and opulent, but I imagine that it may look as though I'm trying to cover my breasts with two lemon wedges.

"Maybe something else?" Zoe says, mirroring my uncertainty.

I pluck a corset from its hanger, a black, lace-up contraption that looks like it is trying too hard to be sexy. I would love to be the kind of girl who could pull that kind of thing off, but when I've tried on anything like this before I look like something from the Rocky Horror Picture Show, and I feel like a fraud. It's just too much, or perhaps I am not enough for that kind of style.

Eventually, I find a deep purple lace and satin lingerie set that I like, and can envisage myself wearing for a romantic session with Matt. The bra is a balcony cup that barely contains my curves. The panties are French knickers that flatter my hips and cover the roundness of my belly and bottom. I may be an apple-

124

shape, but I plan on looking mouth-wateringly delicious.

Zoe comes with me to a little mirrored changing room, and I try on the bra and pants.

We have been naked in front of each other so many times, throughout our whole lives, from splashing around as toddlers in her paddling pool, to changing at P.E. in school, to sharing the trials of puberty, and on into adulthood. I don't even think twice about stripping off in front of her. One of the things I have learned from working with pregnant women is how diverse naked bodies can look, and how we are each different, but essentially all the same. This gives me a little more body confidence, but I am still nervous about taking my clothes off in front of a new partner for the first time. It's normal, that fear. I'm sure it's normal.

"Perfect," Zoe says, as I parade up and down the changing room in the purple set.

"You don't think the pants are too much?" I ask, still eager for Zoe's opinion and approval.

"They are perfect for you. He will love them."

She knows. She knows as well as I do what my thoughts are. I beam a smile at her and change into my ordinary clothes.

As I get to the cash desk and reach into my bag for my purse, my phone is glowing with the notification of a received text. Of course, it's Matt. I quickly click and read it.

I had a good idea! How about a walk and Sunday lunch in a nice pub before your shift tomorrow? My treat xx

It sounds idyllic. I love walking through the woods, by the beach, through the park, anywhere with great scenery and good company. I remember being with Adrian, and seeing other couples linking arms, wrapped up in each other, as we walked feet apart. I longed for that couple-y closeness that we never had. I picture Matt taking my mittened hand in his, leading me through autumn leaves, treading the path through the greater gardens. We could stop in the Hedgehog Café in the park, drink hot chocolate and watch the dog walkers. I dream of the day we have our own little terrier, plan a future. I'm off again, imagining a life. The life will have to wait. The Sunday morning I foresee involves me catching up on sleep, rolling out of bed at eleven, gorging on croissants and coffee and reading my book until I have to force myself to head to work at two. There will be other Sundays. Sundays when I am not working, when I truly can relax and enjoy Matt's companionship.

Zoe nudges me; I'm at the front of the queue and the sales assistant is reaching out her hand for my card.

"Sorry," I say, juggling my purse and phone. The total is over thirty pounds, so I pass my card to the lady.

"Matt?" Zoe says, nodding towards my phone.

"Uh huh. He's so sweet," I smile.

The shop assistant wraps my lingerie in tissue paper and throws in some scented beads, then hands back my debit card.

I go to put my phone back into my bag with my purse, but Zoe puts her hand on mine.

"You can reply, it's fine. I'll go and pick up some tights while you message him."

I'm sure she would have said before if she needed them, and I feel like she is giving me the gift of these minutes to message him without feeling guilty, but I am grateful. I reply to his text.

Sounds lovely. Can't do tomorrow. Another time for certain. xx

The terrier, the drinks in the café, the mittens in mittens, they have all faded from my mind already. As if he knows that I only have a short time to message him, a response arrives immediately.

Before work? I'll have you back in plenty of time? xx

It's so lovely of him to have thought of this idea, and I'm very grateful for his offer, but I'm not going to change my mind. Much as I needed Tuesday evening to chill on my own, I also need tomorrow morning to relax.

Sorry.

I tap in the word and leave it hanging there while I think of what to say. I feel a little like a parent telling their child that, no, they can't open their Christmas presents yet, they have to wait until the twenty-fifth. He certainly is insistent, and persistent. Still, I am saying no. There's the tiniest part of me that thinks maybe I should relent and give up my planless plan to accommodate him. What am I going to do, really? Nothing. But that's the point. I want to be able to do nothing, and not to have to answer to anyone for it. This is the hangover from two bad relationships. I want to make my own decisions, and I want to not feel bad about sticking to them.

Sorry. We must definitely do this in the future. Such a sweet idea. Not tomorrow though. Hope you understand xx

Almost as soon as I have sent the message, one arrives in return.

Understood xx

That single word, but still the kisses. I can't begin to gauge his tone or his mood based upon that response. If I have angered him or annoyed him with my resistance, I don't know.

Zoe stacks three packs of tights onto the counter, and pays the sales assistant.

"Everything okay? Say 'hi' from me," she says, but I don't.

CHAPTER TWELVE

My Sunday morning is just as I planned it. The alarm wakes me at eleven, and I lie in bed, scrolling through the internet, reading nothing in particular, and watching lame videos on Facebook. Eventually I drag myself to the kitchen, still in my fleecy penguin-print pyjamas, brew coffee, and stick a croissant into the oven. I would be lying if I said I didn't think about Matt and the morning that we could have had. As I stir milk into my coffee, I imagine the hot chocolate at Hedgehog Café. As I sit and read my book, I lose concentration, drifting off to an imaginary hand-in-hand walk, kicking through leaves. Still, I'm happy in my pyjamas, content in my home, and looking forward to having my date with Matt on Wednesday. I haven't worried yet about how I will play the evening. I could ask Zoe, but perhaps I'll go with my gut. Perhaps following my instincts is what is best for me.

Zoe. I click through to my messages to write a text. I want to ask her about Theo, but I think better of it. There's every chance that Luke could read the message. I could phone her, maybe send her a Snapchat. It's not something I would usually do but, there are ways to creep beneath the truth and cover one's tracks. I know this because Zoe and I have talked about it. I know this because the guy before Adrian taught me about the ways someone can hide in the digital shadows, cover their tracks, avoid being caught out. Zoe told me where to look, what to look for, how to find him out. Now it is her who is sneaking slyly. Now I am an accomplice to the act of dishonesty. I like Luke. I like him a lot, but my loyalty will always lie with Zoe.

I send her a quick message:

How are things? What's new?

It's a couple of simple questions, leaving everything in her court. If she starts to talk about Theo then I know it's safe to discuss it with her. I'll know she's keeping her secrets safe. If she doesn't mention him, then neither will I. We can talk more when we see each other on Monday.

I think about messaging Matt, but the pangs of guilt are back again. I still feel bad about not meeting him today, despite having had a perfectly pleasant morning on my own. There's definitely some truth in what Zoe said about learning to enjoy my own company and doing good things for myself. I can't remember the last time that she was alone, she's been with Luke for so long that I'm sure she's probably forgotten too.

By the time I've had breakfast and showered it's almost time for me to leave for work. I've put on my orange underwear. It feels autumnal and reminds me of the Pumpkin Spice latte I had yesterday, and then of the walk through the leaves that I could have had this morning. I don't have time to dwell on this. My shift starts in twenty minutes, and I have to go.

Sundays are typically the quietest days on the ward. There are no elective operations, and, as GP surgeries typically don't open on Sundays, we have very few referrals. The only women who are sent in to us come from community midwives, who work a rota over the entire seven days of the week, and will pop in to see women regardless of the day. If any potential issues are detected, we get a phone call and a new patient. There are only four women in the whole of the ward when I arrive for my shift, and three midwives working today to care for them. It is not common for this to happen, so I plan to enjoy the downtime, and also to input some time into checking the cupboards and cabinets in the store rooms, making sure we have enough of everything we need and that none of the equipment packs are out of date. We have cleaners on the ward daily, but I plan to give everything the once over when I've finished with the stocktake. I can make a quiet day into a busy one, no problem.

After dinner, I am just winding down for the evening when a lady is sent in from *community*, which is basically what we refer to everything outside of the hospital as, to be monitored.

I meet the woman at the door to the unit, and she starts talking as soon as I introduce myself.

"My community midwife came out this morning, just a routine visit. I was a bit worried about baby not moving enough, and she said to keep an eye on it, count the kicks today, and pop in if I was still worried."

"Okay…" I take a look at the handheld notes that she has given me. "Michelle?"

She nods to confirm.

"And how many kicks have you felt today?"

"Hardly any. I've been quite busy. We were decorating the room, putting up wallpaper. Have I been overdoing it?" Her face is stricken with worry.

The front page of her notes says that she is thirty-six weeks pregnant.

"Do you feel like you have been?" I show her into the assessment room. "You've had quite a straightforward pregnancy so far. Low-risk." I'm quickly leafing through her notes, and there's nothing that stands out. "I wouldn't recommend getting up any high ladders, because your centre of balance can be thrown off a bit while you're pregnant, but, in general, it should be fine. What I'll do, if it's okay with you, is to have a feel of your belly, and have a listen in to baby on the monitor for half an hour or so. Have you been monitored before?" I gesture towards the cardiotocograph monitor.

"Yes," she says. "In clinic. It was all fine."

"So you understand what the monitor does and what we are looking for?"

"I do, yes. You'll check the pattern of the heart rate to see how baby is?"

"Yes, that's right. It gives us a good idea whether baby is happy, looking at the rate and the pattern, how it reacts over time. It should go up and down a fraction from the baseline and accelerate when the baby jiggles about. I'll give you this button to press too, and if you feel any movements from baby while you are being monitored, could you press that, please?"

She nods and sits up onto the bed. As I palpate her pregnant abdomen and place the cold blue-gelled pads onto it to connect to the cardiotocograph machine, I feel the baby kicking at me.

"That's good. Did you feel that?"

She grins and nods again.

"Excellent. Okay, I need to quickly check your blood pressure and pulse, and then I'll get you a drink. Tea, coffee? Water?"

"I'd love a tea. Thanks."

The trace from the monitor is as reassuring as the kicks from the baby, and within the hour Michelle is ready to go home again.

"I'm sorry I wasted your time," she says.

I shake my head rapidly. "It's never any trouble. If you're ever worried, or if you ever feel like baby isn't moving as much as he…she…?"

"I don't know yet, we didn't want to find out."

"As much as baby should be, then you just give us a call and we will get you back in," I say. "Anytime. Okay?"

She gives me a relieved nod and takes her handheld notes from me. I see her out of the ward, and then go back to the office and write up her maternity record just as the night shift midwives start to arrive. Work days can be like this. I might never see Michelle again, but I have had the opportunity to provide care to her today and to give her the reassurance that she needed. Sometimes women come and go, sometimes they stay with us. Sometimes their memories linger and the emotions that we feel persist, even after they have physically left the ward.

I get home at around ten and can't find the energy to do much more than watch some Netflix and cover myself with a fleecy blanket on the sofa. I'm setting my alarm for the morning when I realise that Zoe hasn't replied to my message. She hasn't even seen it. I stare at the blue bubble that holds my text, and the tiny circle next to it that shows me that the message is still unread. I guess that she must have gone to bed early, I click my alarm on and head to sleep.

CHAPTER THIRTEEN

The ward is still quiet when I return in the morning, but that all changes when I receive a phone call from a GP who wants to send in one of his patients.

"I have a patient in my antenatal clinic," the GP says, "Mrs Claire Cavendish, Twenty-nine-year-old primigravida, thirty-two weeks with unbearable backache, difficulty walking." I can hear him flicking through her paperwork before he adds, "query early labour."

The local GPs are mostly appropriate with their referrals, but *query early labour* usually means that they have assessed the woman, and they are not completely confident that they can reassure them that everything is fine and send them home from the surgery. The last thing that a GP wants is for a woman to go home and end up giving birth to a premature baby on the kitchen floor, or more commonly on the toilet, because they misdiagnosed them. Referring to the antenatal ward is a safety precaution for GPs as much as it is for woman and babies. Of course, the well-being of the mother and child is paramount, but it would be foolish to think that the ever-looming threat of legal action and patients suing the NHS doesn't influence caregivers' decisions now.

"Sure, you can send her in, and I'll let the consultant know. Who is she under?"

That rustling of paper sounds again as the GP looks for the information.

"Curtin. Hospital number 567433."

"Thanks," I say. "Please remind her to bring her notes and we will see her soon."

Claire arrives within the hour, hunched, one hand on her back, the other clutching her husband's arm. She's groaning softly with every movement forward, so I admit her to the room closest to the entrance. It's a four-bedded bay, and I pull the curtain around us to give her some privacy.

"I'm Violet, one of the midwives on the ward. I'll be looking after you today," I say. I don't want to state the obvious, but I have to. "You look like you're in a lot of pain. What's been happening?" I've had the handover from the GP, but I want to hear it in Claire's own words.

"Pain," she says. "Lots of pain. It's just getting worse. I thought it was just normal. I know that backache can be normal in pregnancy so I kept thinking it would settle down and get better. It's right in my back, here." She turns slightly to show me exactly where the pain is centred, on her spine, about ten centimetres above her buttocks.

"I can see it's intense. Does the pain come and go or is it constant?"

"Constant. It's been that way for…" she looks at her husband. "Three days? Four? I didn't want to trouble anyone but then I started to worry. It actually probably started a couple of weeks ago. Maybe more. I waited as long as I could, but I can't bear it anymore."

"Okay. I'll need to check you over and have a listen to baby's heartbeat, and I'll call a doctor to come and have a talk to you, see what we can do. Have you had pain relief at home?"

"Paracetamol. Ibuprofen. That's all I had. About an hour ago the last ones."

"I can't give you any more of that for now but the doctor will be able to sort out something else for you. You have the pain now?" Another question that seems to have an obvious answer, but I want to try to exclude the *query early labour* if I can.

She nods.

"Is it okay if I put my hand on your tummy? I just want to check you're not having a contraction."

Claire lies back on the bed, and I put my hand gently onto the fundus, the top of her uterus. It's soft. No contraction.

"I can't stay in this position," Claire says. There are tears in her eyes. I pull the backrest up on the bed so she can sit upright and get more comfortable.

Back in the office, I call Doctor Curtin's team, and the senior doctor says he will come to assess Claire as soon as possible. He's happy for her to have some stronger pain relief, so I get some Pethidine from the controlled drugs cabinet with my colleague. It should help. I hope it will.

When the doctor arrives at the ward, I hand over Claire's notes. She's had a straightforward pregnancy until now, nothing to flag up to him. She's not got anything of note in her medical history either. Whatever is happening, it seems like it's something new. It doesn't look like early labour, and she doesn't have any symptoms of a urinary tract infection. There's no blood loss. I'm not sure what's going on, and neither is the doctor. He asks me to take some bloods from Claire, and prescribes her *PRN*, as needed, pethidine along with some suppositories for extra cover. Tomorrow, she's booked for an ultrasound scan.

I expect that we will be keeping Claire in the ward until her pain subsides and we are all reassured that this is not the onset of labour. I am assuming that the analgesia we can give her here is going to be effective. I am assuming that we can make everything better. Sometimes I assume too much.

At lunchtime, I check my phone. Monday is, and has been for as long as I can remember, my coffee date with Zoe. There's still no response to the message I sent her. It's sitting unread. Almost two days, and nothing. Okay. Maybe I'm over-thinking. Maybe something is wrong with her phone. It's been long enough that I can try to contact her again, surely?

Everything okay? Coffee date still on?

Imagine the worst but hope for the best. I send it. What else? I click onto the Messenger app, we rarely use it, but maybe her text messages aren't reaching her, and this could be a simple solution.

Hey. I've texted a couple of times. Phone not working? Are you on for coffee today? Miss you.

It's the truth. I already miss her. It's weird not having her there, at the end of the phone. It's weird not hearing from her. If we don't have our coffee meet up today, it's going to be so very weird not to see her. I never missed Adrian this way. As soon as I made that decision to leave, it was like cutting an invisible tie. I freed myself from him. I had no further longings to be with him. I've never wanted to see him since I left. Not once have I felt the urge to even message him.

I have five women under my care by the time I leave for the day, and Claire seems to have the most straightforward prognosis. I'm more concerned about the second-time mum in bed three who is teetering on the edge of preterm labour at twenty-eight weeks. Her first baby was born early, and all the signs are pointing towards baby two being a copycat. I hope she will be here tomorrow, and I hope I'll be able to discharge Claire home. The pethidine seems to be easing the pain a little, but Claire still has some discomfort. The ultrasound scan should answer some questions, and give us some idea of how to proceed.

When I finish my shift, I've received a message from Matt, but still nothing from Zoe.

How's your day, gorgeous? Sorry we couldn't see each other yesterday. Hope we have lots of long walks and romantic lunches together xx

That's still on his mind, but far from mine. I didn't want to revisit the guilt of not having met up with him. Still, he seems to be taking it the right way. Perhaps I can relax just a little.

Despite not having heard from Zoe, when I leave the hospital, I head to Coffee Express. I don't expect her to be there, so I'm not surprised when she is not. I order a Pumpkin Spice latte, and sit in the same seat, drinking that same drink that I drank here on Saturday with my best friend. I'm treating myself to some carrot cake, its lush sweet buttercream compliments the coffee, and cheers me up a little after the long, tiring shift and the Zoeless afternoon. Our Monday tradition goes back years, being here without her feels a little surreal. There's a gaping hole where she ought to be, on the chair opposite me, and in my life. She didn't reply to the message that I sent through the Facebook app. She's still not replied to texts. I figure I should phone her. As a self-professed introvert, I avoid using the phone as much as possible. Of course, it's something that I have to do at work, but that's midwife-me, and she's confident and professional. Everyday-me *hates* using the phone. I don't even phone my mother. Still, I flick onto my contacts, and click Zoe's name, making the call.

My phone trills out the sound that lets me know it's ringing, trying to get through to her. The screen says *Connecting...* but it does not connect. She doesn't answer. If she can hear it, if she's receiving my messages, she's definitely ignoring me.

I stick my fork into my carrot cake, but I no longer have an appetite. The coffee and cake don't have the same taste without the correct company to eat them in. I miss Zoe. So much.

I could text Matt, tell him I'm free tonight, invite him over, but I don't. The space left by Zoe isn't one that he can fill. I don't need romance. I don't need sex. I need my friend. I need Zoe.

CHAPTER FOURTEEN

Tuesday, back on shift, I only have one C-section to scrub for, and then I'm sent back on to the antenatal ward. There are two other midwives on shift, so they've been busy so far without me. It's ten thirty when I get to the ward, and they've already been around with the drugs trolley, checked blood pressures and pulses, and listened to fetal heart beats. My colleague Sarah has been caring for Claire whilst I've been off the ward, and she gives me handover of her and two other patients.

Claire has an appointment in ultrasound at eleven-thirty. I ask the support worker if she can escort her down to the scan department, but she's been asked to go and help out on postnatal, where they're short-staffed, so it looks like I'm doing it myself. It's fine. I like the continuity.

"Sarah, can you keep an eye on bed three for me, Mrs Dawes, while I take my lady to scan?" I have the whiney tone of apology in my voice that comes from the strain of understaffing.

"Okay, no problem."

Sarah smiles, and carries on writing her notes. It's never any problem for us to help each other out. We are used to making do with what we have - or who we have - available. Being flexible comes with the job.

So, at eleven fifteen I fetch a wheelchair for Mrs Cavendish, slip her notes into the slot in the back of the seat and wheel it to her bedside.

I arrive to find her standing, leaning over, one hand on the bed and the other rubbing her back.

"Hey. You okay?"

"The pain. It's so bad now. I had the tablets that Sarah gave me. It's getting too much now."

"Is it the same pain as it was before? Constant? In your back? Doesn't come and go like contractions?"

"Just the same. Just worse. Same kind of pain."

I flick my eyes up to the ward clock and then pull her drugs chart from the notes.

"Your appointment is in ten minutes. I can get you some more pain relief before we go if you need it?"

She nods. I put my hand onto her arm, gentle, reassuring.

"Be right back," I say as I go to grab Sarah to sign out some pethidine with me. It takes two of us to issue the really good stuff.

By the time I've got the pain relief ready and got back to Claire we are already running late. The drugs won't kick in for a few minutes, but we have to be on our way. I'm satisfied that the pain isn't early labour, that she has the same pain that she has been experiencing up until now, only worse, as she says.

"Happy to head down there and see what's going on in there with the little one?" I say, gesturing to her belly.

"I wouldn't go as far as saying I'm happy, but yeah, let's get on. Seeing her will be something to cheer me up at least."

She settles into the wheelchair and I try to navigate the corridors and lifts in a way that causes the least amount of discomfort to Claire.

It's fifteen minutes past her scheduled scan time when we finally arrive.

"So sorry," I say to the ward clerk, who takes Claire's notes from me and runs down her list for the appointment. "Claire is in a lot of pain. I had to get her an injection before we came down. We're a bit…"

"Late, yes. Don't worry about it, I'll get you in as soon as I can."

The clerk smiles and gestures over to the seated area.

I could hug her, if there wasn't a desk between us, and if it wouldn't be totally inappropriate and awkward. Waiting can be such a time sink. My mind is still flitting back to the ward, to Sarah watching over Mrs Dawes, and my other patient. I know she can handle anything, but that doesn't stop me feeling bad about my absence.

I wheel Claire over to the seats and we chat while we wait for the sonographer to be ready for her.

Just before noon, a blonde lady with the lilac coloured uniform of a sonographer calls us into the darkened room. I push Claire through and help her up onto the couch. The pethidine has had ample time to work by now, and whilst she's not entirely pain-free, Claire is a lot more mobile.

"Hi Claire, I'm Astrid," the sonographer says. She sits on her stool in front of a machine with a large keyboard, tracker ball and two screens, one of which she angles towards our patient.

"Hi," Claire says, instinctively looking at the screen although it's still blank.

"So, you've been having pain?"

"Yes. Started a few days ago, just here." She puts a hand beneath herself to her back. "And I thought it was just normal pregnancy pain, you know, but then it got the point I couldn't take it anymore. So, I went to my doctor and he sent me here." Repeating the same story to different clinicians is part-and-parcel of being a patient, it seems.

"Doesn't look like early labour from what we can see," I tell the clinician. "There's not been any bleeding or anything but if you could have a look at the placenta and see if anything is going on in there?"

"Sure." She looks at the radiography request that the obstetrician has sent with the notes. *Abdo. pain. ??Abruptio placenta.* Even though there hasn't been any sign of blood loss, sometimes the placenta can come away from the inside of the uterus slightly, causing pain that could manifest in a way similar to that which Claire is experiencing. Because the obstetricians don't know exactly what is causing the backache, they are looking to exclude possibilities. Diagnosis is like searching for clues. Some are clues to what is going on, some are clues that help us to rule out what isn't happening.

The sonographer turns to Claire.

"So, I need to get to your abdomen, please."

Claire is wearing pyjamas, loose jersey pants with a waist-tie and a T-shirt top emblazoned with Winnie the Pooh having some issues with a honey pot on his head. She tugs up the top and pulls down the pants to rest below her bump, just above her underwear.

"You've done this before!" Astrid smiles. "Okay, this is going to be cold." She squirts blue conductive gel onto Claire's bare belly, and Claire flinches slightly against the chill.

"Let's see what's happening."

Astrid traces a white plastic transducer over Claire's abdomen, running through the blue gel like a toddler's hand through finger-paint.

Every now and again she stops to click her keyboard and take measurements of the contents of Claire's uterus. I've seen enough scans to recognise parts of the baby. I could point out the head and the limbs, the general outline of the fetus, and its position. Beyond that I don't know much else about the fuzzy black and white blurs that the sonographer is investigating.

Claire is lying, looking at the screen, smiling at the image of her baby. Despite the pain, she has some comfort in seeing her future child.

"Excuse me a moment," Astrid says. She turns off the machine, puts down the transducer, and leaves the room.

Claire looks to me for an answer that I don't have.

"Is this normal?"

I shrug, impotently. "I'm not really an expert," I say. "I'm sure she'll be back in a minute."

Three minutes pass that feel like thirty. The door opens and Astrid comes in with another lilac-uniformed woman.

"Sorry about that," she says. "I wasn't sure what I saw. My colleague, Mischa, is more of an expert in this kind of thing, so I'll get her to take a look, if you don't mind."

Claire says no, but my mind is snagged on the words "this kind of thing". Astrid has been an obstetric sonographer for as long as I have been working here. Five years including the time I spent as a student midwife. I'm pretty sure she's an expert. She puts the transducer back onto Claire's abdomen and moves it around until she isn't pointing at the baby at all. She is aiming it at something though. Not baby. Not placenta. I know what those things look like, and that's not what she's showing Mischa.

Instinctively I reach for Claire's hand.

I have a dull, sick feeling in my own abdomen. I need to sit down all of a sudden, and I find the chair by Claire's side before I start to sway.

I know. I know before Mischa speaks. There's something wrong here. It's not placental abruption. It's something worse.

Claire looks at me, and sees my expression, and that's the first time her expression changes too.

"What is it?" she asks. "Is something wrong with the baby?"

"Baby looks absolutely fine," Astrid says, but her face remains unsmiling.

"We are going to need to have a chat with the doctors." Mischa turns the screen back to Claire. "This," she says, pointing at an area of dark shadow, above the baby, behind the placenta. "This is not supposed to be there. I think this is probably what's causing you the pain. Please, I don't want you to worry, we need to investigate further and find out exactly what's happening here, but…it appears that you have a tumour."

CHAPTER FIFTEEN

By lunchtime, an hour later after I expected, I'm ready for a vodka, never mind a cup of tea and the dull salad I prepped last night. It's not happening to me, I know, it's not my pain to bear, but I'm in a state of shock all the same. I pick my bag up from my locker and pull out my phone. The screen shows notifications for the usual messages from Matt, a couple of emails and nothing else.

I press my thumb to the pad to unlock and go straight to my Messenger. The blue text boxes sit unseen by Zoe. My iMessage is tagged *sent* rather than *read*. When I get into stressful situations, she's always the first person I turn to, but now, who do I have? What can I do?

I click onto Zoe's Facebook profile to check whether she has posted anything, but there's nothing new. I shake my head and ask myself what the hell I'm doing…and then what the hell she is doing.

Having an awful day.

I type and then delete. For the first time in my life I think *she doesn't care*. My head is a fog of Claire and Zoe and Matt and confusion. I stick my fork into my limp lettuce, guide it into my mouth and chew. It is tasteless and flat. The dressing has started to turn the leaves to mush. I can't face any more, so I put the lid back on, and wash my mouth with the lukewarm tea.

I want to browse through Zoe's Facebook some more but I can't bear it. Seeing her face, seeing our faces smiling there together, it's too much to take. Instead I read the new texts from Matt.

How's your day? Can't wait to see you tomorrow xx

Busy, beautiful girl? Message me when you're on break. xx

Standard but sweet. That sums up our relationship. We send each other cute messages, we have date nights and dreams of cosy days. There's no criticism, no controlling. Sweet, yes. Refreshing. If Adrian was absinthe, then Matthew is a traditional

158

lemonade. The heavy, straw-coloured mix of tangy and sweet. Basic, but dependable. You know where you are with lemonade. Adrian intoxicated me, made me something other than myself. He made my senses swim, and I thought that I liked it at the time, but I know how toxic that intoxication was.

When I return from lunch break, a tall, smartly dressed lady that I don't recognise is sitting on the edge of Claire's bed.

"Doctor Harrison," she says, holding out a hand to me. "Consultant oncologist."

Oncologist. The word makes a lump form in my throat. A cancer doctor. She must see my shock, as she adds, "Doctor Curtin asked me to review the ultrasound and come to see Claire. We don't know exactly what we are looking at yet…"

She trails off, but her tone is expectant, like she is waiting for me to say something.

It clicks.

"Sorry, yes. Violet," I say. "Staff midwife Cobham."

Doctor Harrison nods and turns back to Claire and her husband. "We need to book you in for an MRI scan to find out what we are dealing with."

"But isn't that dangerous for the baby? Can't you see what's in there with the ultrasound?"

"We can see that there is something there, something that shouldn't be, but ultrasound is quite limited as a diagnostic tool. Basically, we need to have a better look at it."

"And is it safe?"

"We only do it when we really need to, of course. It's…pretty much safe. The need to carry out the investigation overrides any small safety concerns, Claire. An MRI will not harm the baby."

Claire nods and squeezes her partner's hand. He looks down to her and speaks softly.

"We need to do this, love. We have to find out what's happening. I need you to get better. I need you."

"The baby…" Claire starts to reply, and he leans to hug her, speaking quietly into her ear. I can't hear what he says, but she nods her head slowly and turns to the doctor. "Yes. Okay."

"Until we have the MRI results, I can't answer many more of your questions. We need to see exactly what the tumour is, where it is…we need information that we can only get from the scan. As soon as we have that I'll be able to talk to your obstetric team and we can all discuss the way forward."

Claire is silent, but there are tears rolling down her cheeks.

"It's such a lot to take in, I understand," Doctor Harrison says.

I pass over a tissue, and Claire dabs at her face.

"I never even thought…I mean…I assumed it was just something to do with the pregnancy. The baby growing, pressing on my back, something like that. Then it carried on and I was worried there was something wrong with her, or that I might go into labour or…" She shrugs. "I never imagined this. It's like the absolute worse case scenario. You know when you have a cough and you google your symptoms and worry you might have bubonic plague? This is that. The most unlikely, surreal…" Tears are streaming down her face now, and she wipes them messily with the tissue.

"It's not *surreal* though. It's real. It's actually really happening to me."

"To us. We are in it together," Michael says. This does nothing to staunch the flow of tears.

Doctor Harrison smiles and puts her hand onto Claire's arm. "You will need each other. And we are going to do everything we can to support you through this."

I have been on the sidelines of this exchange, standing, numb and dumb. What can I say that is of any use? What can I say?

By half past three I'm a wreck. The mental and physical exhaustion pull me down like a weighted jacket on a scuba diver. I keep kicking my legs, trying to rise up, but the more I try, the heavier I feel. I'm looking forward to being at home, leaving work behind.

I press my thumb against the home button to turn my phone on and click through to my messages. There's still nothing from Zoe.

No more messages from Matt either. Perhaps there's something wrong with my phone. I do what anyone would do – turn it off and on again. The signal strength shows me four bars, everything seems in order. I tap out a message to Matt.

Not long now. Looking forward to it too xx

I know he will send a swift reply if my phone is working, and he doesn't disappoint. The little dots flash up to show that he's typing, and his response flashes up in hardly any time.

Been a long day. Wish I could see you tonight! Would love to feel your cuddles xx

I smile at his message, and then frown knowing that my phone is definitely working but that Zoe hasn't read or replied. Cuddles are what I need too. The warm presence of another person. Comfort. Security. That's what I need.

I didn't tell Matt about not seeing Zoe yesterday and I haven't told him that she has not replied to messages. Somehow, I don't feel like I know him well enough yet to open up, to share my troubles. I want to focus on positive, happy things. I don't want to introduce problems. My mind flits from my day at work to the fact that Zoe is MIA. I pick my phone up at irregular intervals to check whether Zoe has replied yet. Each time, of course, there is nothing.

I think about how I would even explain to Matt that I texted Zoe and that she didn't reply, but even thinking about writing it makes me realise how dumb it seems. It's been just over two days, I shouldn't be worried yet, but for some reason there's a tiny niggle, a crumb of doubt that I can't swipe away. This simply is not like Zoe. Something must have happened to make her unable to message me. Something must have happened between her and Luke. It's the most obvious answer, and as they say, if it's the obvious answer, it's probably the correct answer.

I put my phone down again and try to stop thinking about it. When I try to focus on something else, my thoughts switch to work, and Claire.

I try to relax, but my mind is swirling with speculation. The more I attempt to distract myself, the more I think about what could be happening. If Zoe needs me, she knows where I am. If she needs time alone to work through something, I can understand that. I just wish she would contact me.

CHAPTER SIXTEEN

On Wednesday, the last thing on my mind is seeing Matt. I need to talk to Zoe. I want to offload some of the stress from work. I want to know that she is okay. I want to know why she hasn't replied. I swap out my morning in theatre with Carly, one of the other scrub-trained midwives, so I can spend my full shift on the ward with Claire. I want to be with her for her MRI, I want continuity for her, but in all honesty, I want it for me too. I want to know what's happening. I want to know that she is going to be alright. I want so much but nothing seems to be going my way. I hate myself for having that thought, when I know what Claire is going through, and when I have no idea what Zoe might be experiencing. Stupid selfish Violet. Stooopid stooopid stooopid.

As it turns out, Claire can't get an MRI scan until tomorrow. Outpatients sometimes have to wait months to be scanned, so even tomorrow is fast. Her baby is moving well, its heart rate has been perfect on the cardiotocograph traces and Claire has adequate pain relief for the time being. The anaesthetist has set up a morphine drip for her, which is making her sleepier but reducing her backache.

Before Michael arrives on the ward, I go to sit by her, for a few quiet minutes.

"I can only imagine how you must be feeling," I say.

"I don't know how I'm feeling really." She shuffles in the bed, bringing her legs up so that I can sit beside her. "Still in shock. Me and Michael. He's been great, but…I don't know what to say to him either. I know he's terrified."

"You must be too?"

"But I'm scared for him as well as for me. I'm scared of how he's feeling, how he's coping with this. I'm the strong one." She forms a small smile that is filled with sadness. "I don't know what he would do without me."

I suck in my breath. "I don't think it's going to come to that. I don't know. I mean. Wait for the MRI. We'll know a lot more after that. But don't start thinking the worst. Not yet. Not now."

"It's all I can think. I can only imagine the worst, because then, if the worst doesn't happen, then I'm lucky. Then something good has happened. If I pretend everything is going to be fine, then surely I can only be disappointed."

I nod, knowing that this logic makes some kind of sense.

"Find out more. Get more information before you believe in the worst. Your scan is tomorrow."

"Tomorrow feels like a thousand years from now."

I'm questioning my abilities as a midwife, a caregiver, a supporter. I don't have the words to magically make Claire feel any better. I can't do anything.

As if to save me from floundering for something useful to say, the door opens and Michael walks through. He heads straight up to Claire's bedside, kisses her softly on the forehead and gently hugs her. He does so much more than I ever could, and yet it still solves nothing.

I'm home by four, tired as usual. I've had so much on my mind today that it's been difficult to focus on my date with Matt. I should be nervous, excited, or both about him coming to my flat for the first time. Instead my head has been a muddled mess. I have to prepare the flat, prepare dinner and prepare myself. It's going to be a rush.

I decided on the menu as soon as I'd invited Matt over, so I'm not worried about cooking. It'll be my speciality: pasta carbonara, garlic ciabatta, and leafy salad so it looks like I'm trying to be healthy. Dessert will be Ben and Jerry's because I can't cook any puddings that taste anywhere near as good as Cherry Garcia ice cream. I have everything I need. Dinner is going to be the easy part. On to the cleaning.

I start in the living room, picking up empty mugs, a jumper I'd left on the armchair last night and my trainers, which are already trying to hide under the sofa. I have this cute lamp that I found in a second-hand shop in town, which is a stuffed pigeon under a glass dome that is illuminated by a warm vanilla-glow bulb. It's twee and tacky but I love it. I flick off the ceiling light and switch to pigeon power. The dimmed light gives a more romantic, ambient feel, and hides the fact that I didn't take time to dust or hoover.

I don't have a plan for whether I'm going to be showing Matt my bedroom and the contents of my underwear, but I figure I should at least make sure that both are tidy. I throw my dirty clothes into the wash basket, stack the books that I'm currently reading on a neat pile on my bedside cabinet, and sweep everything off the top of my dressing table into a drawer. "Ta-da!" I exclaim to the empty room.

It will take me twenty minutes to make dinner, so I reckon I have time to bathe rather than shower. I kick off my clothes in the bedroom and turn on the taps, filling the bath with hot water and a squirt of strawberry bath foam. I wash my face, plaster on a creamy mask, and slide into the tub. Much as I want to see Matt, I could just lie here in the hot water for the next two hours and then tumble into bed alone.

I let my mind wander to our date, to keep me from thinking about the terrible week I've had as much as to revel in the anticipation of the night ahead. If I let myself, I would obsess about Zoe and what the hell is going on. Think about Matt, think about Matt. I think about Claire. I think about the tumour. I think about her lying there, worrying about her future. I think about how crazy everything is and wonder how I'm meant to concentrate on being with Matt, having a good time, when all I can think about is work, and Zoe.

My phone beeps from where I left it in the living room and I know that it will be Matt. He's trying so hard, giving me so much attention, and what am I giving in return? Carbonara. Ben and Jerry's. Me. Maybe me.

I run the soapy sponge all over myself and when I've had enough of stewing, I get out, dry myself and wax all the important places. I can determine how long it has been since I was intimate with anyone from the time it takes me to do this. Weeks. That's how long.

I towel dry my hair and then sit in front of the mirror at my now-clear dressing table. My brown hair will dry naturally to soft curls if I leave it, so I work on my make up. The scent of strawberries floats around me like a fruity cloud as I sponge foundation over my skin, add a little blusher, plump my eyebrows with mascara and smack my lips with that plum lipgloss that I love. It'll have worn off as soon as I eat my pasta, but

I'm starting out with the right intentions. Applying my make up is surprisingly therapeutic, and my mind is completely focussed on the task in hand.

When I've finished preparing myself, I head to the kitchen and start preparing dinner. I'm just whipping together egg yolk and cream when my phone beeps again. I forgot to check the message that had arrived while I was in the bath, so when I pick up my mobile from next to the pigeon lamp, there are two notifications. Both from Matt.

Tonight is going to be amazing. Do you need me to bring anything? Can't wait xx

Setting off now. Be with you in ten. Let me know if you need anything xx

Luckily for me they are messages that don't really need a response. I do wonder, for a moment, what the *anything* is that he thinks I might need. A bottle of wine? Some secret ingredient for dinner that maybe I forgot? Condoms? I suspect my last guess might be the correct guess. I don't *need* to respond but I do.

No thanks. I have everything. See you soon xx

I have everything, whether we need certain things later or not. I am prepared.

Matt shows up bang on time, holds out a bottle of wine, and simultaneously, awkwardly tries to hug me. I reach for the bottle and step sideways into his hug. If I was feeling tense, my muddled welcome has broken some of that tension. I was. It has. I laugh and invite him in.

"How's your day been?" he asks, settling onto my sofa, his eyes roving around the room, hungry for the details of my life.

"Busy. Stressful." I remember that I don't want to be too negative. "Standard," I add, smiling. "It's pretty much always like that."

I'm still standing up, hovering nervously. He pats the sofa next to him, inviting me to sit. It's almost as though I am a guest in his home, rather than he in mine. I remember that I am the host.

"Drink? Can I get you a drink?" I say.

"Sure. Pop that wine open," he says.

"You're not driving?" I ask. As far as I know, he doesn't live on my side of town.

"I'll just have one." I try to read his expression. Is he disappointed that I'm not already assuming he will stay over? I can't tell.

"Okay," I say, throw him my best smile, and head into the kitchen to heat the pasta and pour the wine.

Over dinner he tells me about a new building he's working on, just round the back of the Coffee Express in town.

My first thought is that I could pop in there before one of my mate dates with Zoe, my second thought is that I might never have coffee with her again. It must show in my face.

"Something wrong?" he says.

I twirl my fork in the fettuccini and shrug. It's too early to involve him in my problems.

"I'm fine. How's your pasta?"

He doesn't reply, he just looks at me, as if I hadn't spoken.

174

"What?" I ask.

"What is it?" He sets his cutlery onto his pasta bowl and watches me. There's no avoiding this, I have to say something.

"Just a lot on at work," I semi-bluff. "I have this patient, this lady, who...she came in with backache and it turns out she has a tumour. Shocking, really. Awful." I look down, carry on eating my pasta, don't make eye contact.

"Sounds it. Yes. Awful. Will she be okay?"

I shrug again. "We don't really know yet. I hope so. She's only twenty-nine. It's her first baby. Her and her husband, so excited about starting a family, and then this happens. Ugh. I can't even imagine."

I'm sure my story has convinced him. It's not a complete lie, I am distracted by thoughts of Claire. Of course, it's not completely the truth either.

"You shouldn't bring your work home with you. It's a burden on you. Such a price to pay for caring so deeply. Things happen sometimes that we can't control. People do things that we don't understand."

"What?" I think I've misheard him. I haven't mentioned Zoe, but that last sentence, it felt like he was taking about her. I'm paranoid, must be. I feel my heart rate start to increase. If I don't calm it, I'm going to have a very unattractive panic attack, and end up with my face flat in the fettuccini.

"Things happen to people, that we don't understand. Sometimes there are no reasons, nothing for us to grasp on to." He reaches a hand across to me and gently strokes my cheek. "Try not to think about it."

I nod. He's right. He's more right than he knows.

I finish my dinner with more enthusiasm and less distraction, and after we've eaten, we head back to the sofa.

It's not long before his arm is around me, and his lips are on mine. My body welcomes his touch, but my mind can't seem to focus. As he kisses me, I think of Zoe and Theo. Zoe and Luke. Zoe abandoning me. I can't relax.

"Try not to think about it."

The words echo in my thoughts again, but I can't stop. I just can't.

I pull back.

"Too much?" he asks. "Too fast?"

"Yes, a bit," I say. "I'm sorry. It's lovely. You're lovely. I just…I have so much going on at the moment."

He makes an exaggerated move backwards on the sofa, away from me, and holds up his hands.

"It's okay. You don't have to explain anything." His smile is so sweet, so reassuring. I'm starting to fall for him, I realise. Right at this moment, I know I'm falling.

"Thank you," I say.

"That woman from work? Still on your mind?"

I'm about to say yes, and take the easy way out, but looking into his eyes, seeing that caring tenderness, I want to tell him everything. So I do.

The words spill out like water bursting through a breached dam. I tell him about how the messages just stopped, how much I miss her, how empty I am without her in my life.

"You have me," he says. "I'm here for you."

I want to tell him that he doesn't understand. He can't understand. He can't replace her.

177

"Thank you," I find myself saying. "Thank you."

And then, with the weight of my secret released, I finally relax into intimacy with him. His lips search for mine, and I let him find them.

When Matt leaves, I have a throbbing sense of emptiness that I have never experienced before. I feel completely alone. I stretch out on my bed, like a starfish, beached. The darkness falls around me, but tonight it suffocates rather than calming me. I'm drowning in my own thoughts. Stop stop stop.

I shake myself, almost literally. Pull myself back from the brink. Time for Plan B. I need to find out if Zoe is alright. Deep down I know that if anything was seriously wrong, Luke would have contacted me. He would have found a way. Still, I have to reach out to him.

I don't have Luke's number, I've never needed it, but we are Facebook friends, so I have him on Messenger. I click on his image, or more accurately I click on the image of Zoe and Luke together that he has as his profile picture. It's a photo from their holiday to Paris, they are at the top of the Eiffel Tower, with the city lying like a blanket behind them, just in shot. I pause as the picture becomes larger on my screen. The two of them smiling at me, looking for all the world like the perfect couple. His arm around her shoulder, her clinging tightly to him. One moment trapped in time. Was she seeing Theo then? Was she wishing that Theo was with her instead of her being there with Luke? Were the smiles and the closeness all for show, or were they genuinely in love? How well did I really know Zoe? How well do I really know her? Why was I thinking of her in the past tense, as though this woman trapped in pixel form was a friend I had once known everything about, and now was unable to reach. It's eleven thirty. Maybe it's too late? Maybe it's just too late. Still, I type

I haven't heard from Zoe. Is she okay?

I send the message and look at the photo again. I stare at the screen, in case he's holding his phone, and ready to instantly reply, but it's wishful thinking. There's nothing. I'm on my own.

CHAPTER SEVENTEEN

My sleep is deep and long. I don't have to be back in work until the afternoon shift, so I didn't bother setting my alarm last night. I'm woken at just after eleven by the beeping of an incoming message on my phone. It's a message from Luke.

She's fine.

That's all it says. Two words. **She's fine.** Far from reassuring me, those two words make me worry more.

Can you tell her I'm worried about her?

I type, and then delete.

My thumbs hover over the keypad on my phone as I decide what to write.

Do you know why she hasn't messaged me?

No, that's no good. I sound crazy. Interrogating Luke about Zoe's intentions. There's still that shred of doubt in my mind that maybe something has happened between them.

Are you okay?

I send.

I'm fine too.

The message comes back more quickly this time.

I don't know what I was hoping for when I decided to contact him, but it wasn't this. If there is something happening, if Luke knows about Theo and they are stuck in some kind of matrimonial mess, my messages are not going to be welcome or wanted. I feel like I'm treading a fine line between appearing concerned and appearing crazy. Say the wrong thing and perhaps he will stop responding to me too. Catch 22. I sigh and put the phone back onto my bedside table, pull the duvet over my head.

I arrive on the ward for handover at half past two, and have to sit through the reports on nine other women before I hear the latest updates on Claire. I'm a professional, I don't have favourites, but because Claire's situation is so unusual, and so serious, I want to know what's going on.

"Room three, Claire Cavendish," the handover midwife says. Claire has been moved into a side room for extra privacy. It's not something that we can do for everyone, as we only have three side rooms on the entire ward, but we allocate them to people who are likely to be with us for long term, or have particular need.

"You all know the history?" she asks, looking at the afternoon team, and we nod. "Okay, well, Claire went for her MRI this morning. I have the report here, and it needs to go to ward seven for review by…" The midwife checks the notes. "Doctor Harrison. We have her blood results here too, so whoever is taking over please get those down there as soon as possible."

"How's she been?" I ask.

"They're still in a state of shock. Husband has been here all day."

"Michael," I say.

"Yes, that's right. Sister has given him open visiting." We only usually allow visitors to the ward at set times. In the hospital as a whole, patients need rest, time to recover, or at least not be made worse by an onslaught of guests. Here, it's not so much of an issue. We have some women with us that are genuinely unwell, like Claire, but just as many who we are keeping for observation for various reasons.

"Fair enough. What's her pain like?"

"The morphine infusion seems to be helping. CTG was fine, baby moving normally, no concerns there."

Despite the pain and physiological stress that Claire is suffering, and the opioid drugs that she needs to receive, the baby appears to have been unaffected.

Handover continues, and the morning shift leave us to our duties. I check in on the two other women that I am responsible for this afternoon, and then I head into room three.

"Hi Violet," Claire says, as soon as I walk through the door. She manages a sleepy smile.

"Good afternoon." I return the smile, and greet Michael too. "How are you both feeling?"

"This drip is really helping with the pain," Claire says, pointing to the infusion. "I could sleep all day though."

"Morphine will do that to you. How was the MRI?"

"Noisy and claustrophobic. I thought I wasn't going to fit in with this big lump."

"I need to take the report down to the…" I am about to say 'oncology' but the word sticks in my throat, and instead I continue with "…medical team. They will have a look and then I expect they'll want to have a chat with your consultant here. I'll make sure that I keep you updated as soon as I know anything, but Doctor Curtin or one of his team will come in to see you later, I'm sure."

"I never saw him for any of my antenatal appointments. His name was on my notes as my consultant, but I've only been into the clinic here once, and I saw some other doctor, not him."

"His team are all very good. To be honest though, you don't really need to see a doctor at all unless your pregnancy is complicated."

"Well, it's definitely that," Claire says. "I can't quite believe what is happening."

"Do you see this often? Do the ultrasounds show up…bad things frequently?" Michael asks.

"I'll be completely honest with you. No. It's not something that I have seen before. I mean, we see the kind of things that we were looking for when you went for your scan, problems with the placenta, or maybe too much or too little fluid around the baby, sometimes problems with baby itself, but…it's quite rare for scans to show…"

"Tumours," Claire completes my sentence.

"Yes," I say. "You have a great team looking after you, Claire. I'm going to go and see Doctor Harrison now, and I'll be back really soon so we can talk about next steps."

Claire nods, and Michael rests his hand onto her thigh in a gesture that looks close and comforting. Sometimes there aren't any words that can make a situation better, but the touch of someone who loves and cares can help.

I grab the case file from the desk in the midwifery office and head off to ward seven. I actually have to check the signs on the hospital walls for directions. It's not every day that a midwife has to visit the oncology ward. Ward seven is a couple of floors down and along several long samey corridors. I squeeze past beds being transferred between wards, some empty, but some bearing patients. An old woman lies sleeping in one, as a porter and a man in the deep blue of a ward sister's uniform transport her to her new destination. Near the entrance to one of the general medical wards, there's a bustle of visitors who have just been let in to see their friends and relatives.

I finally make it to ward seven and press the buzzer to speak to a staff member so that I can be allowed in. Security is a big issue in hospitals. Anyone from the general public can walk in off the streets and around the corridors, but the wards are generally secured with intercom or digitally-coded entry systems.

A crackled voice asks who I am, and then grants me access.

There's a quiet, serious air about this ward, compared to what I am used to in maternity. Even though we have women with disorders and difficulties, the general feeling is still light and positive most of the time. I rub my hands with alcohol gel out of routine rather than necessity, I'm not going to be interacting with any of the patients here. I walk down the corridor to find the doctor. One of the support assistants comes out of a side room, carrying a bundle of linen, and I try to attract her attention.

"I'm looking for Doctor Harrison," I say. "I've come down from maternity." I point towards my lanyard and name badge.

"Just down there, love. At the desk." She hurries off to discard her load, and I head towards the desk she has indicated to me.

There's a man standing next to the nurses' station, leaning in towards Doctor Harrison, deep in conversation. I try to catch the doctor's attention as I walk through the ward, but she doesn't see me. The man seems familiar, which is strange because I can only see his back. Tall, russet-red brown hair, smartly-dressed. I stop dead in my tracks as the realisation hits me. It's Matt. Even without seeing his face, I recognise his poise, his messily styled hair. It is Matt.

"Excuse me love." A voice from behind me alerts me to the fact that I'm blocking the corridor. A curly-haired, portly porter is trying to manoeuvre a bed down the ward, and I am standing slap bang in the middle.

"Oh, Sorry!" I say, shuffling out of the way.

Matt either hears the porter or hears my voice because he turns around.

"Hey stranger," he says. He doesn't seem surprised to see me, even though it's not very common for midwives to frequent the oncology unit.

Seeing him stand next to Doctor Harrison, I can see the family resemblance and I almost laugh at my stupidity in not recognising it sooner. They have the same expression as they regard me in my gape-mouthed surprise. Their eyes are identical. Their bemused smiles are identical too.

It feels strange, sometimes, being able to share smiles in such a sad environment. Behind closed doors, in curtained bays or in solitary side-rooms, patients are attached to tubes, sedated with morphine drips, fighting the tumours that are attacking their bodies. In the corridor we share smiles at this cute coincidence.

In other circumstances I might have laughed out loud, shouted over, and run to embrace him. Here, I give a reverent little wave and walk slowly towards his mother and him.

I should have worked it out, perhaps, but without the side-by-side comparison I forgive myself for not having put two and two together.

Doctor Harrison looks at me, as if waiting for an explanation, and I try to work out which one of us is out of place in this scenario. Is it Matt or is it I? Of course, I know that he's been to visit his mother before, that's what he was doing when we first met, but I didn't exactly expect to see him on the ward. Me? I'm just doing my job. Nothing unusual about that.

"Mum, I guess you know Violet?" Matt breaks the silence before it becomes awkward.

"I do. And how is it that you know each other?"

I don't know Dr Harrison all that well, but I do know her well enough to be aware that she's joking with him. He doesn't seem to get it though, and his face glows blood-pack red.

"Violet is my, I mean we've been…dating," he says, sounding like a kid who has just been rumbled with his high school sweetheart near the school gate.

Dating. I guess that's what you could call what we have been doing. Dating has consisted of surprisingly few dates so far. Blame my schedule. Blame my desire to spend quality time alone. Still, I smile and nod.

"I didn't realise," I say. "Duh."

"It's certainly a small world," the doctor says. She's not smiling, and it discomforts me. Perhaps she is trying to be professional; standing here on the ward in her scrubs and white coat. I've only ever seen her looking serious, maybe it's her default setting.

Matt leans to peck me on the cheek, and it's my turn to blush. It doesn't feel appropriate to be kissed here. Not just on this ward, but in the hospital, in my uniform. As it's not my day for theatre, I'm wearing the standard issue hot pink starched midwives' dress. Pink isn't my favourite, but I wear it well. At least I like to believe that's true.

In some ways the uniform helps me to be someone else when I am at work. Not that I pretend to be anything other than who I am, but midwifery isn't always smiles and happiness. I've never been involved in a case like Claire's before, but there have been other experiences that have deeply affected me. Cases. The uniform, the vocabulary. They are defence mechanisms. I don't want to disrespect any of the women or families that I care for, I don't call them *cases* out of any kind of disrespect. It's emotionally distancing. These words I use, the persona I link to the uniformed version of me. Professional Violet can get changed into her day clothes and go home leaving the *cases* behind. Mostly. This time it's so difficult.

When I was training to be a midwife, I spent some time volunteering at a suicide prevention hotline. There, we went one step further than changing clothes for our shifts, we were given a new name. Partly to avoid any issues with anyone recognising us, although I'm sure that if anyone knew me that they would know my voice, regardless of whether I told them my assumed name instead of my real name. Partly though, it was to aid this emotional distancing. I was Elizabeth when I was there. Elizabeth listened to the phone calls from men and women on the edge. Elizabeth listened to the heavy breathers and dirty talkers, for there were surprisingly many of those types of callers. Whether that was because it was a free phone number and the callers knew that the volunteers aren't meant to hang up on them, or whether it was because those types of callers needed help just as much as anyone else, I don't know. Either way, the detachment and the distancing were intentional.

Midwife-me steps away from Matt, just one small movement.

"Not here," I say, quietly, only for his ears.

He nods and smiles.

"Sorry," he says. "I'll leave you two to talk business. Thanks, Mum." He leans to kiss her cheek now and she leans to receive the peck. "See you soon."

He winks at me in a cheesy way that makes me turn tomato, and heads off towards the exit.

"Small world," Doctor Harrison says.

I shrug. "We met in the cafeteria here, so not that small. He was coming to see you then too."

"Hmm, he does that. I think he gets bored easily. Needs the attention."

"It's all quite new." The notes I'm carrying feel heavy in my arms, and I turn her focus to them, away from my relationship - or whatever it is - with her son.

"So, I have Claire Cavendish's notes for you."

"Of course," she says, and I'm not sure whether she's referring to the newness or the notes. She reaches over though, takes them from me and starts to leaf through them.

"Thirty-two weeks? I'm going to need to talk to the obs team. She's under…" She checks the front of the patient's antenatal records to find out who her consultant is. "Curtin. Okay. Ray, yeah?" I nod. "I'll need to talk to Doctor Curtin to see what we can do about operating. What she really needs is surgery, but with baby still on board, there's no way we can operate. I need to assess her, see how advanced the tumour is, try to work out how quickly it is growing, what effects it's having."

She pulls her glasses out from her lab coat pocket and reads through the most recent reports in Claire's file.

"You know, I'm sure, that pregnancy almost feeds cancer. It causes the tumour to grow more rapidly. All the hormones…the body is a prime site for nurturing these nasty bastards. And there's an increased blood flow. The circulatory volume in pregnancy is greater, the vessels more dilated."

I nod. I have no medical training, I wasn't a nurse before I was a midwife like some are, but I know the basics. I did know about the change in circulation. I know that Claire is in trouble, and we are going to need to deliver her baby. We. The team. I'm determined to be there. I try to remember to keep midwife-me and everyday Violet separate, but I'm emotionally invested in this and even my uniform isn't going to help me now.

Doctor Harrison picks up the phone and dials Curtin's pager. While she waits for him to respond, she questions me further about the patient.

"Mrs Cavendish was putting on a brave face when I went to see her this morning. What has she said to you?"

"She's terrified, obviously. I think she's still in a state of shock. Do you imagine anyone really expects something like this to happen? Pregnancy, having this baby, it was going to be one of the happiest times of her life. And now…this." I don't mention that I'm in a state of shock too. That I've never been through anything like this with one of our patients. I keep my focus professional, my face emotionless.

The phone rings and Doctor Harrison answers. "Ward seven. Yes, hello Doctor Curtin. Mmm. Yes. What's the soonest you can deliver? No, we really must. Okay, yes fine."

I take a seat at the nurses' station while I wait for her to finish the discussion. I need to take the notes back to the ward with me. Through a cracked-open doorway, opposite the desk, I can see a woman, not much older than I, sitting up in her bed, bolstered by cushions. There's an IV dripping fluid into one arm, and a morphine pump infusing analgesia into the other. A monitor shows the spiked tracks of her heart rate;

steady, constant. On the cabinet by her side is a huge, colourful bunch of flowers, and a littering of greeting cards. I see these things every day on the maternity ward, and here, they feel strangely out of context. The cards here read *get well soon* not *congratulations* as they do where I spend my working days. It's easy for me to forget, most days, that hospitals are for the sick as well as for the peripartum patients. It's easy to forget, most days, that illness and infirmity don't respect maternity. Pregnancy women can suffer from all the ailments found in the general population, and when they do, things get complicated.

Doctor Harrison sets down the handset and takes out her pen. After she has scrawled across the notes, she turns to me.

"Curtin is going to have a chat with Mrs Cavendish and her partner, with a view to delivering the baby this weekend. I've written my recommendations in the notes, I'll come up and see her after the obs team have finished."

"Thanks," I say. "I'd better get the file back up there."

She hands the brown folder over to me, holding onto it a second too long after I receive it

"I can tell you're a good one, Violet. I hope you'll be good for Matt," she says before releasing it, and smiling.

Be *good* for him or *be good* for him, I can't help but wonder, as I carry the burden back to maternity.

CHAPTER EIGHTEEN

When I get back to the ward, I check in on my other ladies, who are thankfully low risk and have no immediate needs. I put Claire's notes on the desk and then sit, staring into space as the noise and bustle of the ward continue around me. I feel dizzy, dissociated. Everything spins.

"Violet." A voice to my left.

"Are you okay?" Another voice in front of me.

I can feel my heartbeat. I hear a rapid thuck thuck thuck but it's not my heart I hear, it's the echo of a fetal monitor in the bay opposite the midwives' station. It brings me back to reality more effectively than my colleagues' voices.

"Wh-what? Yes. Sorry. I'm okay." I nearly wasn't, but I am. I am okay.

To my left, it's Sarah.

"Have a brew," she says. Sarah is from Yorkshire, and she's a firm believer in the power of tea to overcome all ills. Medically, it's a flawed theory, but psychologically a cup of tea and a chat with my coworker is probably just what I need while I wait for the obstetric team.

It's not long before the consultant arrives. Doctor Curtin is a looming presence. Over six and a half feet tall, heavy set, with a booming voice and matching laugh. There's not likely to be much laughing today, but he has one of those voices that always sound like he's smiling, even when things are serious. It's comforting, reassuring. He comes into the midwives' office before we go to talk to Claire and Michael.

"How's her pain at the moment?" he asks.

"Better since she has the morphine."

"She's lucid though? She's fit to discuss next steps?"

Fit, yes. Ready, maybe. Can you ever be ready to face something like she is facing?

"She's not sleepy," I say. "I think she just wants to know what's going to happen. They both do."

He's flicking through the notes, and doesn't look up, but he nods. "Of course."

Finally, he turns to me.

"Baby is thirty-two weeks. I think we have time to give steroids and book delivery in for Saturday." That's two days from now. "There's room in neonatal. I've talked to Doctor Brooker and he's going to come down and have a chat with the two of them later." Pete Brooker. The paediatric consultant. Sweet guy, always wears a bow-tie and a suit, unless he's in his scrubs. "Then after she's recovered from the section, we'll transfer over to ward seven."

"Is there no chance of vaginal delivery?" I don't think Claire will want to go through that too, but I have to ask, to find out what options there are, so I can support Claire in the best way.

Curtin shakes his head. "I'd be a lot happier if it was a planned section. Her back pain has been extreme and the labour pain is only going to exacerbate that. Then we have a preterm fetus to consider. I'd like to minimise the trauma to both of them. I know we like to avoid operating where possible, but, I don't think it's in anyone's best interests to go for an induction in this case."

I nod, and he closes the large brown folder. "Let's go and see the couple."

Usually when I accompany consultants to see their patients there's an entourage of junior doctors, sometimes the occasional medical students. I respect Doctor Curtin for coming alone today. Such a conversation deserves the dignity of one-to-one communication.

When we arrive at the room, Claire is sitting up in bed, resting against a nest of pillows, with her eyes closed. Michael's seat is pulled up right to the bedside and he has his head down on her legs, so he can rest on her while he dozes too.

Doctor Curtin gently places his hand onto Claire's free leg.

"Mrs Cavendish," he says in a low, gentle voice.

Her eyes snap open and she jumps a little. Sleep must have been a pleasant break from the waking nightmare she's currently living. The shifting of her legs awakens her husband, and they are soon both alert and upright.

"I'm Doctor Curtin, I think we have met briefly before?

"I didn't think we had," Claire says with a shrug. "Anyway, hi."

"How's the…?" Curtin taps the infusion pump

"Yummy," she says, and they both manage a small laugh.

"That's good," Curtin says. "Let Violet know if it's not giving you enough relief, we can talk to the anaesthetists about other options."

"Thank you." There's a look of genuine gratefulness in Claire's face.

"Now, we need to talk about what is going to happen next for you and little junior here." The doctor pulls his glasses out of his top pocket and puts them on. He sets the case notes on his lap and reads them, even though he's already been through them in the office.

"So, I've spoken with Doctor Harrison, who is the specialist in tumours, and she's given me her medical opinion. She came to see you too, I see." Claire and Michael nod. "Okay. The bottom line is that she wants to operate as soon as possible, to give you the very best prognosis. The best chance of freeing you of this pain, and preventing any further complications. And junior is an obstacle to that treatment. It's not possible for the medical team to do much at all for you whilst you're pregnant." Claire and Michael look at each other and nod again. "Baby is not quite term yet, but we have a lot of babies through this hospital born at thirty-two weeks that do just fine. He or she is likely to need a little extra help. The lungs aren't really ready for life outside the uterus yet, but we can give you an injection of steroids that can help them to mature. Baby is likely to be quite little, and might have some problems with feeding, or keeping himself or herself warm, but we can help with that too."

"Will I be able to breastfeed?"

"That depends on a few things." Doctor Curtin gestures for me to continue.

"Baby will be on the neonatal unit for a little while and you'll stay here with us until you're recovered from the delivery. Preterm babies don't often suckle as well as full term babies but you'll get a lot of help and support," I say.

"But it also depends on what medications or treatments the medical team want you to have. Most drugs will pass through to the breast milk."

"I really wanted to feed him myself," Claire says to Michael.

"Let's get you better, that's the most important thing." He squeezes her hand, then addresses the consultant. "Are we looking at a Caesarean?"

"I didn't want to have to have a C-section," Claire says. She looks close to tears, but she's fighting to hold it together.

"I'm sorry, Claire. Hey, you've been through so much," I say,

Doctor Curtin explains to the couple what he told me in the midwives' office and waits for the information to sink in.

"It feels so unfair that this is happening. I just wanted a baby. I just wanted a family. We were going to be so happy together and now I have pain and a tumour and I can't even have a normal delivery or feed my baby naturally. I didn't want it to be like this."

Michael stands and embraces his wife as the tears fall. No one expects something like this. It's so rare for someone to come in with pain and for it to turn out to be a tumour. I've never seen it happen before. It strikes me as I think this that I am *seeing it happen*. I'm not even experiencing it myself. I'm on the sideline, and though I'm vicariously feeling sadness, disappointment, and a strange sense of loss. I shouldn't, it's not mine to own. I can't know how they are feeling. I can try to put myself into Claire's shoes but I don't think I can come close to imagining the depth of her emotion. Sometimes I don't have the words. She has Michael, though. Her husband, her strength.

Once Doctor Curtin has left, I sit with Claire and Michael and make sure they understand everything that he has told them. They do. They understand, but there's still a comprehensible air of disbelief. The shock hasn't started to sink in yet. Neither of the couple can quite believe that something like *this* is happening to *them*. They have more questions about the tumour and what might happen than I am skilled or knowledgeable enough to answer, but as we chat, there's a knock at the door. It's a firm, confident knock, and before Doctor Harrison pops her head in, I know that it is her.

"Is it a good time for me to come to talk to you?" she asks.

"Yes," Claire says quietly. She sounds shell-shocked. I'm not sure how much more she can take.

"Hello, hello," Doctor Harrison says, firmly shaking their hands. "I don't often come to the maternity unit. I expect you don't often see medical doctors. I'm quite normal though, and I've come to have a little chat with you about what's going on."

Claire shifts awkwardly in the bed, and Michael rests his hand on her shoulder.

"I understand that this is a huge shock to you, but – and I know this is very hard – I want you to not worry too much. We can deal with this. Okay?" She waits for Claire and Michael to both nod. "We can do this. Let me tell you what we are looking at and what I think that we should do."

Doctor Harrison perches on the side of Claire's bed as she starts to explain.

"Your tumour is something called a Schwannoma. Like most people, I expect you never knew that you had Schwann cells. Why would you? Most of the time they are just *there*…" She gestures at her back. "…helping your nervous system to work properly."

"I have a tumour in my nervous system?" Claire is almost breathless.

The doctor holds up a hand.

"These kind of tumours tend to be contained. There's a sac around the spinal cord, and in most cases the growth is within that sac. That makes it a lot easier to deal with than more invasive kinds of tumours. Looking at your scan results, I believe that your tumour is most probably benign and should be fairly simple to deal with."

"You can get rid of it? It's not cancer? It's not going to kill me?"

"If it is benign, as I think it is, then the chance of recurrence of this kind of tumour after removal is small. You could well have had this tumour for several years, but the changes of pregnancy affect your circulatory system; your blood vessels dilate and your blood volume increases. We sometimes see a more rapid growth in tumours during pregnancy because of this. Also, your vena cava gets crushed by the growing uterus, which adds to the engorgement of your vessels."

Claire's breathing has become more settled. She's leaning back into her pillow now, listening to every word, trying to make sense of it all.

"So, you can take it out. I'm going to be okay?"

"The most likely outcome is that I will remove the tumour and you will have the same life expectancy as any other woman of your age." The doctor reads through Claire's notes. "Have you been experiencing any tingling in your arms or legs?"

"A bit of carpal tunnel syndrome. That's normal in pregnancy?"

"If that's what you have, then yes, it can be normal. This Schwannoma, though, can cause some numbness or loss of sensation. Even paralysis. That's from where the tumour presses against your spine, crushing your nerves and stopping them from working properly."

"Your hand and arm were numb," Michael says. "You dropped the bowl of peanuts last week, remember."

Claire nods. "Yeah, this side…" She wiggles her left arm. "I guess it's been not quite normal. I didn't even think about it."

Doctor Harrison asks me to get a reflex hammer, and then taps systematically at Claire's tendons, assessing her responses.

"Okay," says the doctor. "That gives us a little more information to work with. The amount of pain that you have been experiencing. The numbness. The size of the tumour. I don't know how quickly it has been growing but your description of how suddenly the symptoms have come on lead me to believe that it is having a spurt. My opinion is that we should be operating as soon as possible to remove the growth."

"What about the baby? Can't we wait? She's not big enough yet. Not grown enough."

"It's a balancing act. You're at the start of your third trimester. Baby is very nearly ready to be born. I've had a chat with Doctor Curtin already, and he's happy for us to go ahead and deliver your baby, if you agree. He's discussed that with you?" Claire and Michael both nod. "These tumours grow slowly, but in pregnancy they can have a growth spurt. If your symptoms have worsened over a short period of time, I think we should catch this tumour right now and stop it before it does anything more serious."

210

Claire nods and looks at Michael.

"Whatever you and Doctor Curtin think is best," she says. Her voice sounds like she is trying to be brave. It doesn't quite mask the abject fear.

"Will she need…" Michael begins, and then continues in a more hushed tone, "…chemotherapy? Radiotherapy?"

"Most probably not. If we can whip everything out, then once we know that the pain is under control and the wound is healed, Claire will be able to go home and get back to life as normal. Or as normal as life can be with a baby to look after." She smiles. "There is a very small chance that you may need further treatment, but from what I have seen so far, I think not. If we operate soon. If we don't give the tumour any more time to grow."

Claire nods. "We should do it." She looks at Michael again. "We should do it," she says to him.

He nods too. They are agreed.

When I arrive back at the small, empty flat that I am trying to turn into my home, I sit at the kitchen table and sob. Most of the women who come to the antenatal ward have complications that have solutions. Many of those solutions involve delivering the baby, after which time both baby and mother have happy outcomes. Sometimes that is not the case. Sometimes there are pregnancy-related issues that can seriously damage the health of the mother or endanger the baby. Sometimes women miscarry or have stillbirths. It is very rare that I encounter anything like what Claire is experiencing. I feel drained, exhausted, emotionally empty, and I need to talk to Zoe. Much as I am enjoying getting to know Matt, this is not the kind of conversation that I want to have with him. He'd just tell me not to think about it, to leave work at work. Also, I don't want to appear to be emotionally dependant on him – or too needy. Zoe is different. We share these kinds of things. Work pressures, stress, worry. We support each other. But where is she now? I need her.

I tell myself that messaging her again when she's clearly not replying is plain stupid. Stupid.

Stooopid. I can almost hear Adrian saying the word in his drawn-out dreariness. What would he have said? Forget about her. Move on. But it's Zoe. I don't remember what it was like to not have her as my friend. How can she just *vanish*?

I have thought about what to do next many times, and I can't bear the wait any longer. I have to phone Luke. I want to talk to him. Text messaging can only achieve so much. I want him to hear my voice. I want him to sense the emotion. I want him to know how hurt, worried, confused I am. I don't have his number, so I'm thankful that Zuckerberg has opened Messenger up to audio conversations so I can Facebook call him.

There it is again, the smiling image of Luke and Zoe in Paris. He still has her photo in his profile picture. That must mean that they are together, surely. If he knew about Theo, wouldn't he have uploaded a different image, wiping her away?

I click on the little blue phone icon and hear the ringing tone. As the trill continues, I wonder whether he will simply ignore the call. Perhaps he has nothing else to say to me. I'm about to give up, when I hear his voice.

"Violet," he says.

"Luke, I'm sorry. I'm so worried about Zoe. I don't understand what's going on. Why won't she talk to me?"

His voice comes back harsh and severe.

"Look, Violet. I don't know why she doesn't want to talk to you. Okay?"

"So, she DOESN'T want to talk to me?"

"That's what you said, isn't it?"

I retrace my words. That wasn't how I had said it, but it was certainly what I was thinking.

"Does she not want to talk to me?"

I sound pathetic.

"This isn't fair. I'm not her intermediary. I'm not your go-between. This is awkward and uncomfortable, and I don't want to be involved. Whatever is going on – and before you ask, no. I'm not saying that something is going on. If Zoe hasn't messaged you, it's nothing to do with me. You need to sort it out for yourselves."

"How can I sort anything out when she won't answer my messages, when she won't pick up the phone?"

"I'm sorry Violet. I can't help you."

I'm about to speak again when the line falls silent. He has clicked to end the call. Please, I say into the silence. Please.

CHAPTER NINETEEN

Friday is my day off this week and I want to use it wisely. That would usually involve staying in bed until eleven, reading a book, going into Cranbourne for shopping and lunch, and meeting up with Zoe for coffee, after she finishes work. Having weekdays off work is blissful. The town centre is peaceful. You can walk around Primark without having to say *excuse me* every few feet of the way. Today, however, I have a plan. I'm going to go to see her at work. I know where she is. I know what time she finishes. I have to see her. I have to find out what's happening, so I'm going.

I get to reception at three o'clock. It's a square wooden-framed hole in the wall, through which I can see an empty office. There are two desks, as well as the counter on the other side of the gap, but no occupants. The doorway into the main school area is secured by a lock that the receptionist has to open to allow access. No receptionist, no access. On the wooden surround is a buzzer like a doorbell, wired into the office. I press my finger to it and wait.

On the other side of the locked door I see a woman walk slowly down the corridor and into the office room. There's a break in my view of her as she moves, and then she comes into my eyeshot through the frame.

"Can I help you?" she asks, as though she expects the answer to be 'no'.

"I've come to visit Zoe Buxton. Mrs Buxton. She's a teacher here?" I say, less sure of myself as the sentences fall from my mouth.

"What's the name of your child?" she says. It catches me off guard.

"I'm twenty-five! I don't have a child here!"

Her tone changes, and suddenly I feel less like a visitor and more like a threat. If there was a panic button beneath the counter, I'm sure she would be reaching for it.

"I mean, Zoe is my friend. I've just come to see her," I say, trying to behave like a normal human.

"Mrs Buxton is teaching at the moment. Do you have an appointment with her?"

"No. Like I said I'm her friend. Do friends need appointments?"

"Friends usually see their friends outside of school hours, Miss…?" She's holding a pen over a scrap of paper that's already full of notes and scribbles.

"Cobham," I say. "Violet Cobham." Then I frown and say, "Just Violet. She's my best friend, she knows who I am."

VIOLET COBHAM she writes in block capitals and circles around it three times. I look up to see if there's a camera above the desk that she's signalling to and shake my head at my paranoia. I stop shaking my head because I know I must sound and look crazy by now. It's a vicious circle.

"So…" I say.

"She's teaching," the woman says. "That's what teachers do. I can call someone to take a message to her."

I might have let it go and left, but her attitude makes me persevere. I want Zoe to come down here and give me a hug hello and tell me she's glad I came here, that she's not been able to talk. I want

218

her to show this old bitch behind the window that I am her best friend, that I'm not some nutter trying to get into a school for some nefarious reason.

"Yes."

She gestures for me to sit on the PVC-covered bench next to the door behind me, so I assume I'll be waiting some time. But I will wait, so I follow her direction and try to make myself comfortable.

I see the woman pick up the phone and a wave of fear washes through me that she might actually be calling security after all. A few minutes later, however, I see her turn and talk to someone who has entered the office room. I can't see who it is from my position on the bench, the window doesn't allow a good view of the interior of the room they are in. I can tell it's someone shorter than she is though and assume it's one of the kids. A slight pang of guilt hits me, as I realise, I've caused this child to leave their lesson to run a message to Zoe, but it's short-lived. If I was in school, near home time, I'd be glad to be released to be an errand bearer.

The woman gestures towards me, and then speaks to the child again, before walking off into the unseeable space behind.

I see the top of the receptionist's head, and I stand up to get a better view of what is happening. She's talking to the small person who I assume is the same child that she sent on the mission to summon Zoe. I can't hear what is being said, but I can see the child looking earnestly at the receptionist and shrugging. As they finish their conversation, the woman moves towards the window and I catch the last few words "…nothing to do with us."

She stands in the frame.

"I'm sorry, Miss…" She looks down at the scrap of paper on the desk and miraculously picks my name from the melee. "Miss Cobham. I'm going to have to ask you to leave."

"What?" I can't believe what I'm hearing. To not respond to my messages is one thing, but to tell your colleagues to ask me to leave? That's really something else. "What the hell?"

"Miss, I'll have to ask you to mind your language." I'm sure she's heard worse, working in a school office, and she's only complaining to make a point. She glares at me as though I've mortally insulted her.

"I want to see Mrs Buxton. Fetch her here now. Bring her here. Get her down here now." My voice is getting louder and the woman steps back from the window and heads towards one of the desks. She picks up the phone, and I know that now she is calling security.

"Please." I change tack, calm myself. "I just want to see Zoe. Please."

"Mrs Buxton does *not* want to see you." She waves the receiver at me like a loaded weapon. "You can leave, or I can call someone to make you leave."

I can't risk getting into any kind of trouble with the police. Not with my job. It sucks, but I have to drop my tail between my legs and leave. Admit defeat.

"Fine. Fine." My face is burning with anger and frustration and the sheer confusion of it all. "Please though, please tell her to get in touch. Tell me what's wrong. Please."

"I'll tell her," the receptionist says in a way that lets me know that she will definitely not be telling her.

"I'm sorry." I turn to the door and leave. I can barely see my way back to my car through the flood of tears that flow as soon as I am out of sight.

I drive home too fast, too careless. My heart pounding, adrenaline flooding my system. I'm not just upset, I'm angry, I'm confused. I can't bear this much longer. I throw my jacket onto the sofa and wrestle my phone from my bag. As always, there's a message from Matt.

Hope you've had a good day off. Any plans for tonight? xx

I don't have plans. I do have work in the morning. I don't care. I don't want to sit here, thinking about Zoe, thinking about Claire's C-section tomorrow. I don't want to be alone. I type

No plans. Come over? Share a takeaway? xx

There are worse things I could do. It doesn't take long for him to reply.

Sure! About 7 okay? xx

Definitely okay.

See you then. xx

I almost ask him to bring wine, but I have to be up at six thirty and it's an important day. I don't want to get drunk and I don't want him to stay over. I'm not ready to share my bed overnight yet.

My hair is still wet from the rain, despite the warmth of the drive home. I stand in front of the bathroom mirror, rubbing at it with a towel, looking at pale-skinned, bedraggled mirror-me. What am I doing, inviting Matt over when I look like this, when I feel like this? Acting on impulse again. That's what I'm doing.

"It's okay," I tell mirror-me, or maybe mirror-me tells me.

I make myself look human, and sit back onto the sofa, phone in my hand. I have to get this out of me before Matt comes over. I have to empty all of the words from my head, all the feelings from my heart. I have to message Zoe. Not just the snappy single sentences, but I have to say everything. I have to end this. Today, this afternoon at school, it was too much. I have to end this.

Zoe.

I type a few words, delete them, and start again.

I don't understand why you are doing this.
I don't understand what I have done wrong.
We have been there for each other through everything, always, and now you seem to have shut me out of your life for no reason.
You must have a reason, I get that. I just don't know what it is.
I only came to the school because I didn't know what else to do. All I want to do is to talk to you, and to know why you are treating me this way. Is that too much to ask?

I meant to keep the tone of the message calm and conciliatory, but I realise as I'm tapping the

224

screen that it's becoming more of a plea than anything else. It sounds desperate, but that's because it is. I don't know what else to do or to say. I don't know how to get through to her. If this doesn't work, what then? Give up?

Zoe has been my friend for so long that I can't imagine what life will be like without her in it. I don't have to imagine, because I'm experiencing it right now. I'm lost without her.

When I have had any problems in my life, I have turned to her. When my parents divorced it was she who supported me. It was her room that I sat in evening after evening when I couldn't go home because home was filled with reminders of how fragile relationships could be and how my father could pick up and leave without even thinking about how it would affect mum, about how it would affect me. And now Zoe was doing the same thing, abandoning me without any explanation. It doesn't make sense. It hits me, as I contemplate this. She wouldn't leave me of her own free choice. She knows, she understands how much it affected me when dad walked out. She understands my abandonment issues. There's no way the most important person in my life would do this to me. Something has happened.

I look at the message that I have typed but not sent. I clear the text box and start again.

I'm worried about you. I know that something must have happened, and I want to help you. I don't know how to help you if you won't, or can't, talk to me. There must be some way that you can communicate with me so that I can help. Find a way. Send me a sign.

I am about to press send when it hits me. If she can't send messages to me, perhaps she can't receive them either. The last messages I tried to send are still hanging, unseen, in cyberspace, not yet marked with the blue 'seen' indicator. I can't go back to the school. I don't feel like I should go to her house. I'll write a note. I can leave it somewhere...or better still, I can get Matt to deliver it to her. Yes, of course. I'll write it, and give it to him, and he can make sure she gets it. Maybe she will even talk to him, maybe she will be able to let me know what's going on. Why didn't I think of this sooner?

I search through my drawer for stationery. I have some notecards that my work secret santa gave me last Christmas. I never thought I would have any need for them. Who uses pen and paper these days? And yet now I am so glad I have them. I am so glad that I can write something that she can hold in her hand. I want her to feel my emotion through the page; I want her to see my handwriting, to know that I am here that I am her best friend, that I can help her, whatever is happening. I pull out a pen and write.

CHAPTER TWENTY

When Matt comes over, we order pizza and settle onto the sofa.

"Want to talk about it?" he says.

I sigh. I didn't want to do this, not tonight, but I end up explaining about what happened at the school.

"And she wouldn't even come to the office?"

I shake my head. I don't even want to say the words.

"Oh Violet. I'm sorry. Sometimes you think you know people, but…"

"I do know her. She's my best friend."

"She was." His two words sound so harsh, so final. He puts our friendship into the past tense, just like that. Two words.

He's stroking my hair, so gently, when I say to him, "Could you do something for me?"

I know he will say yes. He would do anything for me.

"Of course," he says. "What can I do for you?"

"Would you deliver a letter to Zoe for me,"

As I say it, I feel his hand pause, ever so slightly, as it is gliding over my hair. He continues its movement almost instantly, but I've picked up on the missed beat.

"Is that okay?" I ask.

"Do you think that's a good idea?" he says.

It's my turn to pause now.

"I don't know what else to do. Unless you can think of anything?"

Matt swivels slightly to put his mug down on the little side table, and then turns to me, full on. He takes my cup too and places it with his, then takes my hands, holds them together between us. A neon sign may as well have flashed up saying *serious talk ahead*.

"Violet. Sweet Violet. I'm going to say things to you now, and I'm going to say them because I care about you." He looks so earnest, that it's hard not to laugh at the strangeness of his tone. "I'm going to say them because, well, I love you."

This is the first time that he has told me. It feels peculiar, hearing the words from him, but it feels good. I love him too, I think. Perhaps it's too soon for me to say. My face reddens and I sheepishly look away, unable to meet his gaze.

"You don't have to say it back. Not right now. Listen, I...I think that you've tried your best to contact Zoe. You've texted her and called her, you've tried to talk to her through Luke. You went to all the effort of going to the school and look what happened. She could have come down to that office and talked to you. She could have explained at any point what's happening. She could put you out of this..." He pauses for effect, stroking a tear off my cheek. "...this misery. Look at you, Violet. Would a real friend do this to you?"

I shake my head, silently. I needed to hear this. I needed the words to come from his mouth and not mine.

"But..." I begin to speak, but he silences me.

"Don't, Violet. Don't make excuses for her. You don't deserve this. You've been an absolute state, and it's all down to her."

"She wouldn't do this to me," I persist. It hits me, and it hits me hard. Zoe would never intentionally hurt me. "Twenty-two years, we have been friends. Twenty-two years. A whole lifetime, shared. She wouldn't do this."

"She has done this. She is doing this. You're in denial."

He's trying to soothe me, but it's only antagonising me further. Something has happened. Something serious has happened, and I need to find out what. Luke said she is fine, so at least I know that she's not in danger. Or at least I think I know that. I don't know what I believe anymore. Is Luke somehow involved in this? Has something happened between them? Once I would have found that an impossible option, but once I would never have believed that she would ghost me. Once I would never have believed that Zoe would cheat on Luke. Maybe she's changed. Maybe we have changed. Maybe I don't know anything for certain anymore.

I realise that I've already burned several of the bridges that I might have needed to cross to find out what's going on here. I've made Luke think I'm an absolute nut, I can't possibly step foot on school property again, and Matt believes that Zoe is no good, and that I should move on. He doesn't understand. It's nice that he says he loves me, but I need his support. I need him on side.

I lean forward and kiss him, gently, firmly, and then turn to pick my coffee back up. I have to think.

"Violet, please."

"I know you're trying to protect me, but I have to work this out. Something is wrong."

"Yes, something is wrong." Matt stands up and for a moment I am afraid of him, the way that I've been afraid before. Not of him, that's not quite right. I'm afraid because of the reflex reaction that I have to seeing a man tower over me, move towards me, and everything that can come afterwards. But this is Matt. I breathe. I am calm.

"I can't stand by and watch you make an idiot of yourself over her. She's messing you about. She's straight up ghosting you. Have some self respect. Just let it go."

He hasn't laid a finger on me, but it feels like a slap. I hear the words and maybe the tiniest part of me wants to believe him, but the rest of me still has faith in Zoe. Am I going to burn one more of those bridges now?

"I think maybe I need to be alone tonight," I say. I haven't thought this through, it's a spontaneous decision, and I trust my gut instincts. "I'm so sorry. I feel like I've messed you about."

Now it's Matt's turn to look hurt. He's still standing awkwardly over me.

"I need to decide what to do. Sorry. Let's meet up on Sunday. Go for that walk?"

He looks as though he's about to yell at me. I sense the build up, it's something I've learnt to recognise over the years. Instead he takes a deep breath and sighs. I offer the walk as a compromise. He suggested it, he wanted it, and now I want to give him something to keep the peace.

"Fine. Fine. Whatever. You're making a big mistake, Violet. This is not going to end well."

I think perhaps he is right. Still, I have to try. "If you change your mind, text me. I want to be with you. I can come back later."

"Okay, sure," I say, but I know that I need space and time.

As soon as he's gone I sit and work through the options. I read through the letter that I wrote earlier.

Should I send it? I thought that Matt would help me. I hoped he would deliver it, maybe even talk to Zoe, act on my behalf, but I understand that he wants to protect me. He's never even met her and I wanted that to be his introduction? I shake my head at how desperate I've become, and then stop and smile, thinking of how much faith I put in Matt that I would even ask him. A warm feeling washes over me. This is what it feels like when someone cares about you. I haven't really felt this in a relationship before, only ever in my friendship with Zoe. I always felt so safe with her. So cherished.

I rip the paper down the middle, and then again and again until it is scrawled upon confetti that I take to the bathroom and flush into the toilet. A couple of rags remain after the flush, and I see the words *see you* and *hurt* floating on the blue water.

CHAPTER TWENTY-ONE

If I can't see Zoe at work and Matt's not going to take a letter for me I need to think of another plan. Of course I could take a letter and put it through her letter box, talk to Luke, hang around until she agrees to talk to me, but after what happened at the school I'm worried that he could call the police. I'm worried about looking like a stalker, a trespasser, a criminal. I'm worried about my *best friend* making me feel like all these things. It's unfathomable how we have come from being thick as thieves to worlds apart in only a week.

I take out my phone and scroll through the last messages we sent to each other, searching again for some kind of clue. Anything. Did I say something wrong? Did I do something? I try to read between the lines. I think about what she might think, what she might feel, but I can't work out anything that I've done wrong. Fuck I could drive myself crazy thinking about it.

There's one other option that I've been considering. I don't want to say anything else to Luke in case it stirs something up about Zoe's affair, but could I talk to Theo? It's a possibility. He must know what's happening. All I have to do is to work out how to contact him, and what exactly I should say.

I remember the cliché. Someone from work. That's what she had said when she told me about him. Just before I had that panic attack. Someone from work. For a fleeting moment I'm excited by the thought. Then the sinking feeling hits me. I can't go to the school. Those bridges that I burned? Looks like I'm going to end up wading.

What else do I know about him? Surprisingly little. Actually nothing. He's Theo and he's a teacher at Grange Grammar. Perhaps he's not even a teacher. He's Theo and he works at Grange Grammar. And Zoe is having an affair with him. There's that. I can use that to narrow down the field, if at least I can identify some runners.

I make coffee, strong, just a splash of milk, which swirls in the darkness like a nebula. The answers are not held in the stars, but I'm pretty sure that I can track Theo down in cyberspace. Everyone is online. Everything is online. Theo. It's not your run of the mill kind of name. I don't expect there are many Theos working at Grange Grammar. I set my mug on the comedic coaster next to my laptop, open the lid, and begin sleuthing.

My starting point is Zoe's Facebook page. Friends of friends should be visible to me, I reason. I type her name into the search box. Nothing. Not *nothing* as in I can't find Theo. *Nothing* as in Zoe has blocked me. Well, either that or she's removed her profile, but knowing how much Zoe uses the internet and knowing how things are between us, blocking me seems the most likely occurrence.

"Shit!" I say. I lean back on my chair, staring at the screen. "Shit, Zoe."

I don't know why I'm surprised at this development, but it just seems so final. Not only has she closed down communication with me, but now she's also stopped me from looking into her world. I can't see what she's doing. I've been locked out of her life.

Being blocked also means that I can't scroll through her friends list to find Theo. I'll have to try something else

If I knew his last name, that would be a start. Entering **Theo** into the Facebook search bar isn't going to get me anywhere close to finding him. As if to prove this to myself I do just that. **Theo**. There are hundreds of results and I have no hope of picking him from the list.

I know he is called Theo. I know he is Zoe's…what? Love interest, paramour, bit on the side? There must be a better word for it. Perhaps it doesn't deserve a pretty name. Anyway. I know he works at Grange Grammar. That's the only lead I can follow up right now.

Back to Google.

I type **Grange Grammar staff list** into the search bar. The top two results are **Teaching Staff - Grange Grammar** and **Support Staff – Grange Grammar**. Perfect. He must be either one or the other. **Teaching staff** feels most likely, so I click on that link first, and scroll down. Below the image of the school's crest is, as promised by the title of the page, a list that starts with Headteacher and runs through deputy heads, department heads and then various other subject teachers. There's only one problem. The names

238

are listed as the initial of the first name and then surname. I can't find a Theo that way. I can narrow the field though.

T Carter

T Smith

T Lewis

T Brookes is prefixed by 'Mrs' so I can remove her from my enquiries. I speak the names out loud, but quietly, almost whispering them to the screen.

Theodore Carter

Theodore Smith

Theodore Lewis

It doesn't help.

Assuming that Theo is teaching staff, and not support staff, he must be one of those people. I'll start with these anyway, and if I come up with nothing, I'll move onto the list of support staff. I haven't found the answers I wanted yet, but I feel like I'm getting somewhere.

I write the names onto the back of an envelope beside my keyboard and go back to Google.

Theo Carter. Is that going to be enough? It's enough to show me a lawyer who appears to be

American, based somewhere near Chicago. He's young, and rather attractive, but I know it's not him. The other Theo that this search turns up is a teacher, but he's got a double-barrelled name, and lives in Cornwall. Also, he's somewhere in his fifties, and doesn't appear to be the kind of guy that Zoe would be with. He could have recently moved to the area, sure, but I don't think he could have become younger and more attractive.

Smith is next on my list. Theo Smith. Theodore Smith. Almost like the forename is overcompensating for the surname. If my surname were Smith, maybe I'd do the same. My hypothetical child would be a Desdemona or Ophelia. Orpheus or Achilles. I'm warming to Theodore Smith already, and can almost feel the selection bias seeping out of me. I'm going to search until I *make it* be him.

Fortunately, I type **Theo Smith** into Google and I'm greeted by the smiling face of someone who could absolutely be Zoe's love interest. He's olive-skinned, dark haired; he has a Mediterranean look about him. Theodore. Is that a Greek name? Theo...Theos...something to do with God. Well, I'm not one to judge a book by its cover but he

240

certainly makes a good first impression. I scroll down the results page, trying to find some evidence for the decision that I have made that this is he. There's a link to Facebook, so I click through, and see the same photo of the same smiling God. He's based right here in Cranbourne. It has to be him.

"Yes!" I say it out loud, although there's no one here to hear me.

There's an awful lot of information about him here on his profile. When I've got to know him, I will warn him about the dangers of sharing too much online and show him how to adjust his privacy settings. For now, I browse through his photographs, starting with his profile photo history and then onto timeline photos, things that he has shared openly with the world. There's no sign of Zoe, but I reason with myself that if you're having an affair with a married woman it's probably best not to broadcast it publicly on the internet.

When I've had my fill of his profile, I click on the little blue button that opens Messenger and provides me with the tantalising text box that I can use to contact Theo. I've got this far. I've tracked him and stalked him, and now I have him in my sights. I'd like to say that I had a plan for what I was going to say when I found him, but now I'm at a loss. How should I approach this? I'm having second thoughts.

I should have had a plan before I started. I was looking for a window into Zoe's world, but now I've opened it, and had a look inside, I'm not sure what to do next. Theo doesn't know me, although I'm aware of the possibility that he might know of me. Am I hoping that he does or does not?

My fingers hover over the keys. I stare at the small circle that frames his profile picture. That welcoming smile urges me onwards.

I click on *send message* and start to compose the text.

You don't know me, but I'm Zoe's best friend. I haven't heard from her in a couple of weeks and I'm really worried about her. I'm sorry for contacting you but I don't know what else to do. If I've done something to upset her, please ask her to let me know. I need to hear that she is okay. Sorry again.

242

I send it on its way before I can change my mind. I might not have worded it the best way I could have but I can't sit here worrying about choosing the right phrasing all night.

I'm getting used to this waiting game. Wait for Zoe to reply, wait for Luke to reply, wait for Theo. If social media is my drug, then I'm a heavy user. My phone is never far from my hand. I flick back through Theo's Facebook profile, hoping for some kind of sign, a clue that might give me any information about what is going on with Zoe. Places he's checked in, photos he's posted, likes, events…there's nothing.

I browse over to Luke's profile. He's so different to Theo. Theo is definitely younger, and better looking. Luke is such a reliable, solid guy though. I thought Zoe was reliable and solid too, but that doesn't tally with what's happening recently. Maybe Luke isn't either. Maybe I don't know anything anymore. The photo of Zoe and Luke in Paris smiles out at me, and my heart turns to lead.

CHAPTER TWENTY-TWO

I went to bed alone last night, without even contemplating messaging Matt again. I couldn't. Not after the way I messed him around earlier. My heart sinks at the thought of him. Have I messed this up too? Back onto early shift this morning, I wanted the solitude and the sleep last night. Today is more important than ever. I'll be in theatre for Claire's C-section. I want to be alert, and completely *there* for her. I won't be the scrub midwife passing the instruments and running through the checks today. This time I'll be the receiving midwife, supporting Claire and Michael.

I get to work at twenty past seven, ten minutes early for my shift. I want to get into the right mindset for today; I have to psyche myself up. It's going to be a tough one. I head into the changing room and put on a set of pink scrubs, the cotton pyjamas with the drawstring waist and top with its v-neck slit. I fish amongst the theatre clogs on the floor for a matching pair, and slide them on. It's almost like getting into character. I stick a couple of pens in my pocket and put my clothes and bag into my locker. No distractions today. I'm not messaging anyone. Today is for Claire, Michael and their baby. In a way today is for me. Midwife-me.

In the office, I lift the hefty metal teapot and pour myself a mug before I sit for handover.

"Claire's section today," Sarah says, nodding at my scrubs.

She's just coming onto shift too. I'm glad she's here.

"Yeah. Tough one."

She puts her hand out onto my knee and pats it gently, supportively, and I smile.

The night shift run through the events of the past few hours, updating us on the patients, but it's mostly a blur to me. I make notes as usual, but when I look at them afterwards they look like spider-scribble. I just want to get through to see Claire. To make sure she's okay. To start preparing for the birth of her baby.

When I head into Claire's room, she's looking a lot more relaxed than I expected.

"Hi," she says.

I give her my best smile.

"How are you feeling?"

"I'm trying not to think about that," she says. "Being really hungry is helping."

She's been nil by mouth since last night, no food or drink.

"Sorry about that!" I say. It's standard procedure though, vomiting while under anaesthetic can be deadly, so we try everything we can to reduce the risk. That means no cornflakes for Claire today.

"I have to run through your paperwork with you, make sure you've signed your consent form and then get you into your pretty backless dress." I whisper the next words. "I have to shave you too." It's not a full-on removal of the pubic hair, only the top inch where the surgeon will make his incision, but it can still feel embarrassing to the woman, and sometimes to the less experienced midwife. Having worked in theatre so often, shaving women's pubes has become normal to me.

Claire giggles, and I'm relieved by her relaxed response.

"Again, I'm sorry," I say. "So, Doctor Curtin has explained everything that's going to happen this morning?"

I ask her to tell me, rather than explaining it to her, so that I know she understands.

"We go into theatre, the anaesthetist puts me to sleep, Doctor Curtin delivers the baby, you and a paediatrician check the little one is okay, and you take my baby up to the neonatal unit. I wake up and it's all over. I'll have been stitched up and…Doctor Curtin said something about giving me pain relief up my bum like that one I had before and a drip. And I'll get to see my baby once someone can wheel me up to NICU."

She's already talking in the jargon of the hospital. NICU. The neonatal intensive care unit. She's frank in her description but there's no anger or bitterness in her voice, only acceptance.

I nod. "Because you need to have the general anaesthetic, Michael won't be able to come into the operating theatre, but I will make sure that he sees your baby as soon as he can. He'll be able to go up to the…to NICU…with the team and see the baby when he or she is settled. And hopefully he will be back down

248

to the recovery room by the time you're awake enough to know he's there."

"He'll be here soon," she says. "He gets to have breakfast before he comes in though. He's already texted me this morning bragging about his porridge."

We both laugh as I tick through the checklist. She understands the procedure. She's signed the consent form. Blood results are fine for the operation, her platelets and haemoglobin levels high enough to go ahead. I've alerted the paediatric team and the anaesthetic team. Everything is in order. I check her name band as I have done every day since I've been here. Every time I've given her controlled drugs to ease some of the pain of her tumour. Every time I've drawn blood from her. Every time I've hung up a bag of intravenous fluids. I've almost memorised her hospital number, and I do have her date of birth imprinted in my memory. Thirty-first of May, nineteen-ninety. She's twenty-nine years old. Four years older than I, and she's married, pregnant, and has a tumour the size of a tennis ball on her spine. A tumour that has stopped her from having spinal anaesthetic for the Caesarean she's been forced to have before her baby is truly ready to be born. And here we are laughing, despite all this.

While I worry about dating and stress myself silly about where my best friend has vanished to, Claire has to worry about whether her preterm baby will be okay, whether the operation to remove her tumour will be successful. Whether she will need chemotherapy, or radiotherapy. Whether she will recover from this. She should. Doctor Harrison says she should. But if I were in Claire's position I would still be terrified.

"Doctor Curtin will come in to see you soon, and the anaesthetist, Doctor Dickenson will want to see you too. We can wait until Michael gets here?"

She waves away the idea. "It's fine. He doesn't need to see any more doctors. Not yet."

I smile a flat smile, and place my hand on her arm. "It's all going to be okay," I say. I'm not sure either of us believe me.

I sit back at the desk in the office, completing the paperwork, making the appropriate entries onto the computer system and checking that NICU are ready with their staff and equipment. Everything is prepared by the time Doctor Curtin and his junior assistant arrive.

"How is she?" Curtin asks.

I shrug. "She seems ready. Everything's in order here. Bloods were fine. The anaesthetic team haven't been yet."

He hums and reaches out for the notes. I hand them up to him and watch while he reads the blood reports and the chart that shows her heart rate, blood pressure and other biometric data.

"Okay. Okay," he says. He sounds like he's marking homework. "I'll pop my head in. Charles, you come with me," he says to his junior.

The junior doctor walks quickly to keep up with Curtin's long, confident paces. I've only seen him a couple of times before, he's one of the new batch. Consultants stay in the hospital for years, but the junior doctors come and go. The operating theatre is going to be packed today, with the usual operating team and the additional neonatal crew. If there was ever a morning that I needed to be awake and alert, it's today.

"You alright?" It's Helen, one of the other midwives who is going to be scrubbing in theatre today – the job that I usually get.

I nod and raise my mug of tea, as though it's a shield and I'm showing her that I'm protected. She smiles.

"You've looked after room three a lot," she says. "Claire."

"Claire. Yes. I'm feeling a bit nervous excited about today," I say. She will understand.

"Terrible. Finding out you've got a tumour while you're pregnant. Ugh."

I can only nod. What is there to say?

We sit, draining our cups of tea while Doctor Curtin talks with Claire. Professionals together, sharing a quiet moment of reflection.

After Doctor Curtin has finished, it's not long before the anaesthetist and his assistant from theatre arrive. They crossover in the corridor outside the office, and Curtin exchanges pleasantries with Doctor Dickenson. I don't hear what they say, but Dickenson is smiling as he comes into the room.

He nods a greeting and picks up Claire's notes without asking. I haven't had a chance to see what Curtin wrote, but its likely to be standard.

"Bloods look fine." That's what the doctors seem to focus on first. Are the lab reports okay? What's her blood pressure? The psychological well-being seems to come further down the list of priorities, whereas for me, it's at the top.

"Fine. Fine." He is talking to himself as much as anything else, trailing his finger along the words on the page, as though trying to decipher them. He snaps the folder shut and walks towards Claire's room. The anaesthetic assistant follows behind.

"Shall I come in with you?" I shout after them.

Dickenson bats his hand. "No need. Don't worry."

Perhaps he's tired, at the end of a long night shift, or perhaps he is just being economical with his words. I've long since stopped taking personally anything doctors say to me or how they say it. I expect courtesy of course, and always give that in return, but I cut some slack for the tough shifts and ridiculous hours they have to work.

Helen shrugs and smiles.

"He looks like I feel," she says, and I nod.

"Same. Mornings. Ugh."

We chat a little until the door to room three swings back open and Dickenson stands in the frame, saying a last few words to Claire.

"Yes, absolutely. Of course. Whatever pain relief you need we will sort out for you."

I can't see her face from where I'm sitting but I can imagine her smiling at him. That grateful, gracious face. It humbles me.

As I'm the receiving midwife and not the scrub midwife I stay on the ward until it's time for her to go through to theatre. There's a tap on the door at just before eight and Sarah tells me that Doctor Curtin is ready for us.

"Are you ready?" I ask.

Claire looks up to Michael, and he bends down to kiss her.

"I'm ready," she says.

"Come with us, Michael. You can wait outside theatre and we'll bring baby to see you before she goes up to NICU."

The three of us head out of the room to the operating theatre. Michael and I walking, and Claire in a wheelchair, her IV fluids hanging from its pole.

I make Michael comfortable and then we go to join the anaesthetist. This is it.

Claire has a general anaesthetic, as her tumour makes it impossible for the alternative, a spinal anaesthetic to be sited. The paediatric team and the obstetrician and his assistant take their places, and Helen, the scrub nurse, passes the scalpel to Doctor Curtin.

He makes a quick incision across Claire's abdomen, just above the line where her pubic hair would normally sit. Once the skin is opened, he slices through the muscle of the uterus, until we can see the smooth white shininess of the amniotic sac. The junior doctor holds a retractor, a metal tool that hooks the skin and muscle of the lower abdomen down, out of the way, so that Curtin can reach into the uterus and pull out the baby. It's a swift delivery, uncomplicated and trouble-free. I'm standing near to Doctor Curtin with a warm towel, and as he scoops the baby girl up and out of Claire's uterus, he passes her to me.

She's pink, but covered in the waxy cream coating that we call vernix. It literally means varnish, but it's nothing like a shiny hard shell, it's more like goose fat on a swimmer. Because she's a little early she also has a soft fluffy down-like hair covering her body. It will fall away in the next few weeks. At first glance everything looks normal.

I pop baby onto the resuscitaire, the warming platform, where the paediatrician waits to check her over. I already know that there's not going to be a lot of care that baby needs immediately, as she is crying forcefully, and that's always a good sign that a baby is breathing well. We give all babies a score at birth called an APGAR, and Claire's baby is scoring highly, despite its prematurity. Still, she is small, and vulnerable. She will be likely to need help to keep warm, to feed and even though she's breathing well now, she may need some support in the days to come. The paediatrician nods, wraps the infant up, and places her into the warming incubator ready for transfer to the NICU.

"She's looking great," I say, and the doctor smiles.

"So far, so good," she says. "Is the father outside?"

I tell her that he is, and the doctor and the neonatal nurse wheel the incubator out of the theatre, leaving the room feeling oddly empty, even though Claire is still on the table being sutured.

The first part of the operation, the incision and the delivery takes a fraction of the time that the whole procedure lasts for, as the suturing, the sewing back together, has to be done in layers. The junior doctor is working on the stitching while Curtin supervises and Helen passes him the tools needed for the task. I have little to do until Claire is ready to be brought through to theatre. Normally, the receiving midwife would be weighing and measuring the baby, but all I have to do today is to fill in the notes, enter data into the computer and complete the birth register.

I've had time to do all of the paperwork and grab a tea before Claire is wheeled into the recovery room. She's woozy from the anaesthetic, but still manages to smile as I describe the nice parts of the birth to her.

"She was shouting at us as soon as she came out," I say. "Pink and pretty. As soon as you're fit to get out of this bed and into a wheelchair I'll make sure we get you up to visit. Michael's still up there with her, I'm sure he will have photos for you. Oh, and she weighed spot on four pounds, NICU called down to let us know."

She squeezes out another smile, but can hardly keep her eyes open. I sit by her side, monitoring her heart rate, blood pressure and blood loss, checking on the fluid going in and the urine coming out. Everything, obstetrically, is fine. She has a lot more to go through, but everything, obstetrically, is fine.

I get Claire up to the postnatal ward at just before ten, and give the midwife a full handover. I wish I could stay up here with her and carry on her care, but I'm allocated to antenatal ward, and there are other women for me to care for besides Claire. I can't deny that I've become attached to her, and emotionally invested in her case, but I will be a visitor from now on, popping in to check on how she's getting on, keeping up to date on what happens with her and the baby she's named Libby.

"This is where we say goodbye for now," I say, after I've brought the postnatal ward midwife in to meet Claire. "Sophie will be looking after you this afternoon."

Claire smiles at Sophie and the midwife says hello.

"I promise I'll come and see you." I lean in and give her a gentle hug.

"Make sure you do!" Claire says.

It feels so final leaving the room, leaving the ward, and heading back to antenatal. Claire's old room, room three, has already been filled by a lady whose community midwife has sent her in for assessment of her amniotic fluid volume. I have time to meet the women I'm going to be looking after and talk to Helen about the morning's operation before it's half past twelve and lunch time.

By twelve thirty five I'm sitting in the cafeteria, eating lunch. I poke at my lunch and I almost spill my can of cola over my tray as I see Zoe walk past the windowed wall. Her shock of flame-red hair, her bottle-green leather jacket, that way she has of skipping slightly when she walks. I'm sure it's her.

"Zoe!" I shout, not thinking about where I am. "Zoe!"

She doesn't turn around.

I swipe my bag up onto my shoulder and abandon my soup, crisps and drink.

"Zoe!"

I push past a woman holding onto the arm of a middle-aged man, and almost topple her tray to the floor.

"I'm so sorry," I say, but I don't stop.

I can still see her red hair bobbing down the corridor, and I jostle my way after her.

"Zoe! Please."

She's starts to turn the corner, heading down towards outpatients, when I realise. It's not her. I can see her face in profile as she bears right, and the features are not Zoe's. I'm still walking in her direction and as I close in I have to stop myself, put on the brakes, hold myself back. I'm almost reaching out to her. It's not her. Not Zoe.

260

Stooopid stooopid stooopid. I repeat it to myself as I stop dead, heart pounding, mind racing.

I stumble back to the cafeteria, even though I no longer have much of an appetite. I've avoided a panic attack, at least, but my mouth is dry, and my heart is still thundering. As I fall back into my seat, I see Doctor Harrison looking around for somewhere to sit, balancing a tray loaded with a plate of the day's 'special' (lukewarm mac and cheese), a little pot of yoghurt and a glass of water. She's in danger of colliding with a man who's walking very slowly in front of her, stopping every few seconds to tap at his phone. I tend to be more patient with people here in the hospital than I am elsewhere. I don't know what's going on in his life or why he needs to bumble along the way he is, but I cut him some slack on the doctor's behalf.

I think about Matt, and his brief, awkward visit last night, and hope he hasn't spoken to his mother. Why would he have? Could he have?

"Doctor Harrison!" I call to offer her the free seat at my table, and she loops around the man and makes her way over.

"It's hard work," she says. Not sure whether she means the struggle to get from the counter to the table or something that's happened on the ward today, I mumble and nod.

"You can call me Sherrie," she says. "Even without your…thing…with Matt, it's fine. You're not my patient." She smiles, and I relax a little.

"Thanks. I'll stick to Doctor Harrison while we are on the ward though."

She shrugs a 'whatever' and starts to eat.

The mac and cheese looks as anaemic as a patient who's lost five pints of blood. Cafeteria food is aimed perfectly at its captive audience. We don't have time to go anywhere else, so we are stuck with what we can get. The joys of working for the health service.

I don't want to talk business over lunch, we have enough of that during the rest of the day. I decide to chance it, and fish for some info on Matt. She's civil enough with me for me not to worry any more about whether he told her about last night.

"So, is there anything I should know?" I ask. "Any crazy ex-girlfriends likely to come after me?"

Sherrie doesn't laugh, but she does form a tight smile. Note to self: touchy subject.

"Sorry, I was just…I mean, I…"

"Oh Violet, it's fine. To be honest, I've never really MET any of his ex-girlfriends. I know he was seeing someone maybe six months or so ago, but…long hours, busy busy." She doesn't give the impression that this is a bad thing. "Although…there was this one girl. First time I saw them, he was dressed up in high heels and she was wearing a really weird hat…" Sherrie eyes my horrified expression. "Of course, they were six years old at the time."

My face relaxes and I shake my head at her.

"You had me going then!" We both laugh; it feels good to release some of the tension of the day.

"Honestly though, perhaps I haven't been as…available…to Matt as I should have been. Not recently. Not ever, maybe. I regret it, on some levels, but you know what it's like for women." She takes a sip of her water.

I know how some things are for women. I can imagine that training as a doctor and working in the medical profession is a vast amplification of what I have experienced. I work in a woman-centred profession in more ways than one. It's the male midwives or support workers who stand out as *different* in some people's eyes. I also know about pressure and politics and personal relationships. I know about being controlled and I know everything I learned from the guy before Adrian. I wonder if Sherrie's marriage broke down because of the pressures of work-life balance, or if she knows as much as I do about what it's like for women.

I think all of these things, but my response is a nod.

A silence hangs between us, during which time I crunch thoughtfully on the last of my crisps, and think about how different my life must be to Sherrie's.

I haven't checked my phone while I've been at lunch. I don't like to scroll through it when I'm in company, and I figure it wouldn't make too much of a good impression on my boyfriend's mother. Boyfriend. Is that what he is? I'm not sure if we are there yet, but that's definitely the destination. If I didn't mess it up last night, then that's where we are heading. When she leaves the table, I pull my phone from my bag, and on the lock screen is a notification.

Theo Smith sent you a message.

I almost drop my phone as I scrabble to open the Messenger app and see what he has said.

We should talk.

That's it. No suggestion of why or where. No reassurance, no reason. My heart thunders in my chest, I feel my breathing become more rapid and shallow. The edge of a panic attack is creeping toward me. I can't do this now. Not here with five minutes left of my lunch break and a shitter of an afternoon to return to on the ward. I close my eyes. Slow the breaths. Calm. Be calm. **We should talk.** Be calm.

I message him back.

I finish at 3:30 – are you free at 4? Coffee Express in town?

It seems the logical place to meet. It's been the focal point of so many meetings with Zoe, why not with Theo?

Sure. See you then.

It's short and to the point. Nothing else needs to be said now, but my mind is already racing with what might be said when we meet.

Before I leave the hospital for the day, I pay a visit to the postnatal ward, where Claire has been given a side-room with its own bathroom. She can't use it yet, she won't be back on her feet until tomorrow at the very earliest, but it's a highly coveted luxury on this ward, where patients must usually share a two-shower, three-toilet block between eighteen women. I look through the small window in the door and see that she is sleeping. She looks like any other new mother does when they stay here, apart from the absence of her infant. In sleep she is peaceful, pain-free, untroubled. In a few days she will be well enough for transfer to ward seven. Well enough. Obstetrically well.

CHAPTER TWENTY-THREE

I've been to Coffee Express so many times with Zoe that being here now, waiting to meet with her lover, feels very strange. As I order my latte, I hear a voice behind me that sounds exactly like hers.

"Mocha, extra hot, extra shot," the woman says. Zoe's drink. Zoe's voice.

I swing around and knock a bag of coffee beans off the counter. It lands with a thud at the feet of the woman who is not Zoe.

"Sorry," I whisper, face burning with the shame I feel. I'm seeing the ghost of Zoe everywhere now.

Zoe and I usually choose the same table, but I've purposely selected a table near the side wall today. I don't want to sit where we sat. It's almost desecrating the ground. Ridiculous, maybe, but our table is our table. I don't want to sit there with anyone else.   Sitting by the wall, I can hide behind a menu and keep my eyes on the door. I know that I need to keep my cool, keep my emotions under control, my heart rate steady. There's no room for panic attacks today.

As it happens, Theo spots me before I see him. Am I that recognisable that you could pick me out from a room full of strangers? Probably not, but I've seen his Facebook profile photo and he has seen mine too. I don't know what he knows about me. I can't imagine what Zoe might have said. He's standing in front of me before I notice he's there.

"Violet?"

"Hi," I say, trying to stand up to greet him, and banging against the table. Elegant as ever.

"Theo," he says. Obvious, I think.

He's holding a mug, which means not only did he enter the shop without me seeing him, but he also managed to order and wait for his drink before coming over here. So much for looking out for him.

We shake hands awkwardly and sit at opposite sides of the table. He's not quite as attractive as his Facebook photo, but he is certainly above average. His complexion is definitely Mediterranean, but he speaks without an accent. His dark brown, almost black hair is cut short, neat and clean. I imagine that it smells of an expensive woody-musk shampoo. I'm lost in my thoughts when he starts to talk.

"I have to tell you," he says. "Zoe doesn't know I'm here."

"Okay," I say. "Does she know that I messaged you?"

"No. I wanted to talk to you first."

"So, you know what's going on?"

"I do." He doesn't go straight to it though. "This is all a bit...weird...for me. We were trying to keep our relationship on the down-low. No one was meant to know about us. Obviously with Zoe's, er, situation with her husband, the fewer people who knew about us, the better. Then she told you and, well, all this happened."

"All this?" I don't quite understand what I'm hearing. Have I caused something? Zoe chose to tell me about Theo. I didn't drag it out of her. "What do you mean?"

"Zoe told you. You told Matt. Before you know it the World and his wife will know that Zoe is having an affair." He lowers his voice, suddenly seeming over-

270

aware of our location and the proximity of other customers. "And we don't want Luke to find out. Not like this."

"Luke is a really good guy," I say. "I'm not judging you and Zoe, but I would hate for him to find out second-hand about what you're doing. I mean…I'm sorry. I don't know how to say it nicely. I don't mean it like that."

"You don't approve. I get it." He gestures with his hands in a nonchalant shrug. "Zoe wasn't happy with Luke though. She's happy now. We are happy. Isn't that what you want?"

"If she is happy, why isn't she talking to me? What have I done so wrong? I might not approve but I've not criticised her decision. I didn't tell her to stop seeing you. We agreed to support each other. Respect each other's relationship choices." I can feel the tiny prickles of tears start to sting my eyes. Keep calm. Keep calm.

"You told Matt."

I furrow my brow, letting the words settle, not quite hearing them, not quite wanting to. Not understanding. Theo continues.

"Zoe said that you told Matt and that everything was ruined. Everything had to change."

"What does that mean? Why should it make such a huge difference that I told Matt? He's my boyfriend!" I use the word 'boyfriend' more comfortably than I have done before. Matt has been there for me when no one else has. I love being with him. He loves being with me.

Theo regards me with his chocolate brown eyes, not breaking eye contact but not speaking. He shrugs.

"I'm sorry, but I don't understand," I say. My forehead corrugates in a frown. I'm trying to work out what damage could have been caused by talking to Matt about Zoe's affair. He doesn't know Zoe. He doesn't know Luke. "Do you and Matt know each other?" I ask.

Theo's thick, dark eyebrows raise in surprise.

"Why would I know him? No. Of course not."

"I think she's just overreacting," I say. "Matt would never tell anyone about you and Zoe. I understand that Zoe doesn't know him, and I understand that you obviously want to keep everything under wraps. I'd never do anything to hurt her. Never."

"Hey. Hey. Calm down. Ssh." He looks around, as my voice rises, as if he's worried that I'm going to create a scene.

"This is all just so…ridiculous!"

"I can see that you're very upset," Theo says flatly, still trying to keep me from reaching my boiling point.

"Why couldn't she just tell me that she was angry with me? She could have told me that she was annoyed that I had spoken to Matt about the two of you, and I could have reassured her and…" My breath is becoming shallow again. I'm aware of it, thankfully; maybe I can get this under control before I spiral downwards.

"I don't know. I honestly don't know. Look, are you okay?"

I breathe deeply, slowly, in, out, in, out. Slowly. In. Out.

Finally, I have it defeated. I speak.

"Sorry. Yeah. I'm okay." I'm shaking, still not quite in control. "I get these panic attacks. I'm...I'm okay."

"It's hitting you really hard," he says, as though he's just discovered something momentous. "I'm sorry. I wish I could tell you more. I don't know anything else though."

I gulp in a breath and sigh it out again.

"Look," he says. "I'll talk to her. I'll tell her that I've seen you. I'll tell her how hurt you are. This is wrong. It's all just wrong."

I pause, considering this before I reply. Is there any reason why I shouldn't let him do this? I haven't asked him to, he's acting of his own volition. Really, what have I got to lose?

"Thank you." The words fall quietly from my mouth. I barely hear them myself. I repeat them, more loudly. "Thank you."

I'm not sure what will happen next. I'm not sure what I expect. Expect nothing. See what happens. See what happens.

CHAPTER TWENTY-FOUR

I've arranged to meet Matt at the not unreasonable time of eleven thirty on Sunday morning. Yesterday was the stressful conclusion of a stressful week. I'm drained, exhausted, wiped out. If I'm over-using descriptors, it's because I'm feeling over-used. Getting out of the house, meeting up with Matt and seeing the outside world is probably just the remedy I need.

There's no rain today, but from my window I can see that the world outside has a crispness that comes from the chill of autumn cold. I wrap up warmly, and head out for our date feeling positive.

I'm determined to focus on Matt, and to enjoy our day together. Claire's delivery has lifted a little of the weight from my shoulders. I'm still worried about what will happen with her operation to remove the tumour, of course, but knowing that the baby is doing well after her early delivery is a relief. Seeing Theo has also helped me to shift some of the burden I've been bearing. He's going to talk to Zoe. He might even have spoken to her by now. I can only wait and see what might happen next. I can't do anything more than I have done. I don't have any more control. Today, I'm determined to focus on Matt.

The way I treated him on Friday night hangs heavily on my mind. I feel like I used him. I called him over and I dismissed him without any consideration of his feelings. I've fobbed him off, put him on hold, and then when I wanted him, I snapped my fingers and he came. All this, and yet he still wants to see me. He's still as enthusiastic as ever. I never really appreciate what I have.

I sit on a bench by the pier, watching the people walking past, as I wait for Matt to arrive. Two women in sweatpants and hoodies jog past. A man walking a small beige floppy-eared dog is forced to stop as his canine companion pauses to sniff a passing Labradoodle. A couple walking hand-in-hand chat animatedly as they head towards the promenade. Life goes on all around me as I watch the clock and wait.

Matt is five minutes late, but when he arrives, he greets me with a hearty hug that I don't feel I deserve.

"Hey gorgeous girl," he says. His face is beaming with happiness and it's infectious. I grin back.

"Hi you. I'm so sorry…"

He stops me before I can complete the sentence. He presses his lips against mine, sealing my apology within.

"Ssh," he says. "It's fine."

My cheeks glow with the bite of the cold, and the thrill of my emotions. I'm falling. I definitely am.

The date is as I imagined it would be. Matt takes my hand and we walk along the promenade, feeling the sea breeze in our hair, letting the salty air fill our lungs. There's something about it that invigorates me. I can see why people used to come to the seaside to recuperate when they were ill. Today I feel alive, I feel free. I don't have to put on a show of positivity, I'm actually starting to feel it for real.

From the seafront, we head into the gardens, past the miniature golf course and a man juggling flaming clubs. The stench of burning kerosene is overwhelming and I'm glad when we approach the Hedgehog Café, where instead I can smell churros and coffee. We buy both and sit at one of the little round tables, enjoying the sunshine, enjoying our time together.

"We should have done this last week," I say. "You were right."

Much as I like being alone, being with Matt today has made me realise that there is also a lot to be gained in the company of someone that you like spending time with.

"Like you said. No rush. I'm glad we are here now. You seem a lot happier today. Has something happened?"

"A couple of things. The lady with the tumour. She had her baby," I say.

He sips at his coffee and doesn't speak.

"She'll be on the postnatal ward for a few days, and then we'll transfer her down to your mum." I smile. That little connection pleases me in a way that I can't explain. We have something in common, no matter how tenuous.

"She's one of the best oncologists around, or so I'm always told," he says. His voice is emotionless, rather than proud. I feel like changing the subject before I sour our day.

278

"The second thing," I say, between mouthfuls of crisp churro, "is that I messaged Zoe's boyfriend. I met up with him yesterday. He's going to ask her to get in touch with me. I haven't heard from her yet, but I feel like I will. I feel like, I don't know, like something good is going to happen. Like everything is going to be sorted out."

"You did what?" He puts his paper cup down onto the table. His eyes are wild. I don't understand, and then I think that I do.

"I met Theo, Zoe's boyfriend. We had coffee. That's all it was. Nothing for you to be jealous about."

"Jealous. Is that what you think it is? I'm not jealous. Why would I be jealous? I just…" He pauses, his eyes flicking across my face; I can almost hear his brain whirring, trying to find the words. "I think she's making a fool of you. I think you should stop trying to get in touch with her. Like I said, let it go."

"But…I'm so close to ending this mess. I'm so close to getting her back in my life."

He shakes his head, and looks away from me, suddenly fascinated by two dull brown ducks that are walking along the riverbank. I watch them as they waddle along and finally plop into the water.

"I thought you would be happy for me. Happy that I'm happy."

He looks back towards me. "I think you would be happier if you were rid of her. I'm sorry. I can only say it as I see it."

"I understand that, but you have to realise that she has been my friend all of my life, and I don't want to be without her. It's all been a big misunderstanding. You see, Theo said that Zoe was upset that I had told you about them. Silly isn't it? You don't even know them, why should it even make a difference?" I laugh, and put my hand on his, but he pulls away.

"What did he say?" His tone is clipped.

"Just that. He said that Zoe stopped talking to me because I told you about her and Theo. So silly. Once Theo has explained everything to Zoe, I'm sure she will be in touch and we can sort everything out. Life is going to get back to normal." I am beaming, but Matt's face is ice-cold.

"I'm sorry," he says. "I have to go. I forgot, I said I would help Dad with something. I'll text you later."

"What?" I can't quite believe what he is saying. This day, this date, this is what he wanted. Everything was going so perfectly. What now?

"I have to go."

He leans and kisses my cheek with a polite, perfunctory peck, and before I can say anything else, he has started to walk away.

I have a choice. I can get up, run after him, demand an explanation, or I can watch him walk away, and wonder again, why, why, why?

I can't bear any more of the uncertainty I have faced this week, so I choose to leap up and hare after him.

"Matt. Stop! Please!"

He keeps walking, increasing his pace a little. It would feel almost comical if it weren't so embarrassing.

"Please. I'm sorry. I don't understand."

I catch up with him and reach my hand out to take his.

"Matt."

"Violet. Don't. I have to go. Really. I'll message you later. I promise. Have a think about what you are doing with Zoe. Have a think about what kind of life you want. What kind of people you want to give your time to."

"Oh Matt, it's so sweet that you worry so much about me, but really, it's fine. Everything's going to be fine."

He looks at me, bends to kiss the top of my head and walks away. This time, I let him go.

CHAPTER TWENTY-FIVE

I receive a text message, as promised, some three hours later, as I am snuggled on the sofa with my Kindle.

Sorry about earlier. I completely forgot I had made plans with Dad. Hope you can forgive me xx

Matt doesn't seem like the sort of person who would make plans and forget them, but how well do I know him? This morning was perfect right up until the time I mentioned Zoe, and then everything went a little bit nuts, to say the least. I don't understand it, and I'm not even sure I can try to. I assume that he is being overprotective, but that doesn't explain his rapid exit. Perhaps he did have to meet his dad after all.

Okay. Easily done. Don't worry about it. I had a lovely time in the park with you anyway xx

I expect another message back straight away, but nothing comes until much later in the evening.

**Don't be angry with me. I care about you so much.
I love you xx**

Those words again. I haven't said them back to him yet, and I don't want the first time to be via text message. Still, his sentiment is reassuring, and it feels good to be cared about, good to be loved.

I'm not angry. We'll see each other again really soon xx

This time his reply comes more quickly.

Tomorrow? xx

Sure. Why not.

On Monday, I'm in theatre again, back in the role of scrub midwife. The theatre list consists of four C-sections, and I'm on my feet for six hours solid. I don't get my break until the list is done, and by that time it's barely worth heading back to the ward. I finish up paperwork and offer to help the other midwives. Everything is under control.

"You can finish ten minutes early, go on. It's been a busy one," she says.

"Thanks. I'm going to pop up to see Claire Cavendish. Is there anything to go up to the postnatal ward?"

I'm grateful for the early finish, it's a rarity here.

Sister hands me a couple of blood result print outs that belong in files upstairs. There's always some little thing that needs to be transferred.

"Send her our best," Sister says, and I nod as I head off the ward.

Claire is sleeping when I arrive. I stand in the corridor, looking through the small square window into her room. She looks so calm, so peaceful, as if she has no worries in the world. The room looks big and empty without a cot beside the bed. I'm used to having to squeeze between wall and bed to get around these cramped little spaces. I'm sure she would rather have the baby with her, rather than the extra room. Libby. Not Elizabeth, like the assumed name I used to have, just Libby. Straight up, simply Libby. I stand a little longer, looking into the room as though the window is a portal to a different reality. In a way, it is.

One of the postnatal staff midwives taps me on the shoulder and I jump slightly.

"She's doing well," the midwife, Marie, tells me. "We got her up in the wheelchair to see Libby today. Quite a trek with all the drips and tubes, but well worth it. Have you seen her?"

"Not since the birth. How's she doing?"

"Libby? She's doing okay. In the incubator, with nasal oxygen and a feeding tube. Just what you'd expect."

"Little fighter, like her mum." I smile and look in the window again. Claire is going through so much, and I'm struggling to cope with such a minor disruption to my life by comparison.

"Tell her I popped by. I'll come back when I'm next on shift."

"Will do. Anytime, Violet. Try not to take too much home with you. It's not healthy." She grips my shoulder tenderly and I nod.

"I know," I say. "It's difficult sometimes, isn't it?"

"It's difficult often," Marie says.

When I get back to my car, I'm in no fit state to drive. My hands are shaking, in fact my whole body is quivering with exhaustion. I consider for a moment heading back into the unit, going to see the supervisor, talking this out. As a midwife, even though a lot of our work is one-to-one with the woman we are caring for, we are never really alone. There's support for each of us on many levels.

The rain is pounding, more than drizzle now, it's turned into a full-on shower. I can barely see out of the windscreen, and when I see a red-haired woman walking in my direction, I think I'm seeing ghost Zoe again. The skip in the walk, the green leather jacket, the red hair hanging deep scarlet in the rain.

"Stop it. Stop it. Stop it." I can't help myself from saying the words out loud, trying to get my stupid mind to stop imagining things that aren't going to happen.

"Stop it."

But the figure comes closer, heading straight for me, the skip getting faster as the rain bounces off the leather.

I squint my eyes and rattle my key into the ignition, to start the wipers, to clear the windscreen. Before I can turn on the engine, she's tapping at the passenger window.

I must have left my lights on, or dropped something outside, or maybe it's one of the nurses, urgent news about Claire. It's not. It's none of those things. It's Zoe. She's here. It's actually her.

"What the fuck?" I mutter to myself.

She taps on the glass again and I press the button to wind down the window. Rain splashes against the upholstery, bouncing up onto my face, mixing with my tears.

"Violet. I'm so sorry."

"Zoe?" I still can't quite believe it's her. It's almost as though the times I thought I saw her before have conditioned my brain to think that she's just an optical illusion. "Zoe? What…?"

The storm is drenching her, water trickling from her soaked hair onto her clothes and down, through into the car as she leans towards me.

"I never meant to hurt you. I didn't want to…I'm so sorry. Let me in. Let's talk."

"You could have called me or come to see me at home or…"

Zoe shakes her head, resolutely.

"No. I should have come here earlier though. No one can see us here."

I'm not sure what she means as this is a very public place. A hospital car park is full of visitors, staff and even patients, coming and going. An elderly couple walk past the front of my car as I'm thinking about this, looking curiously at the woman standing beside the door, as if to prove my unspoken point.

"Are you going to let me in or what?" she says. "I'm drowning here."

I press the lock release button, and Zoe bundles into the passenger seat, just as she has thousands of times in the past. This time, though, she feels like a stranger. I'm not sure I know the woman who would treat me as she has treated me.

In the past, my instant response to the events of today would have been to text Zoe, to get together with her to drink (coffee or vodka) and cry. Without breaking any client confidentiality, I would explain the pain, and Zoe would help me to feel better. Now, I feel angry and confused.

She reaches across to hug me, and I recoil, pressing myself against the window behind me.

"Okay," she says. "We can save the hug until I've explained things."

The rain falls in heavy round balls against my windscreen, a constant droning thud-splash that I would usually find calming. Unlike most people I love this kind of weather. The pungent aroma of petrichor, the electric buzz in the air before the breaking of a storm. I feel that same tension between Zoe and I now.

She pauses before she begins.

"I really missed you," she says.

"Yeah," I say. "Well, it was your choice to block me out of your life. Literally block me." I add that so she knows that I know. I know she didn't only stop talking to me, but she deleted me from her social media, wiped me out of her life.

"Actually, it wasn't really my choice." Her face bears a sad, serious expression.

"I couldn't risk Luke finding out about Theo and me. I was stupid. I know I was. I've not been happy with Luke for...well, for quite a while. I know I didn't say anything to you, and I'm sorry, but...I was more worried about you. You and Adrian, well it was all such a mess, wasn't it?"

I nod. I understand that maybe I wasn't as open to listening as I could have been. I was tied up in my own problems and I appreciated Zoe listening to me.

"At least I have Matt now." I smile, but Zoe does not. Instead her face is stony, cold and hard.

"Oh Vi. I'm sorry. I didn't want to do this. I know you think you have found someone good there, but Matt is no good for you."

I start to protest. "Not this again. You haven't just come back along to start criticising my decisions?"

Zoe sighs heavily. "It's not like that. I almost wish that it were. If I was just being overprotective or irrational it would be a lot easier."

"Then what *is* it?"

We are skating around the truth like a patch of thin ice that we don't want to get close to. Perhaps we should steer clear. Perhaps the truth isn't what I want to hear.

"The reason I've not been able to talk to you. It's Matt."

"Yes, Theo said —" I start, but Zoe lifts her hand to silence me.

"Not long after you told him about Theo, Matt added me on Facebook. So, I accepted his friend request because I thought that's the polite thing to do, even though I've never met him and all I know about him is that he's your...boyfriend."

"But...he's not on Facebook. I checked. I searched for him..."

"Violet. He is. I'm sorry. He is."

I'm not sure what the truth is anymore.

"As soon as I accepted, he messaged me."

I already have a sick feeling in my stomach. The rain is too loud now, the car feels claustrophobic. Too small, too confined. The world is closing in on me.

"He seemed polite at first. Just your general kind of chat. Asking how I am. Saying how he's heard so much about me. 'Fine,' I thought. Nothing weird about that. Then he started to talk about you."

That thudding thunder. The weight in my gut.

"He likes you a *lot*. But I think that's the problem. He saw me as…somewhat of a threat to your relationship. He told me that he thought you and I spent too much time together. That I was eating into time that you should be spending with him."

"That's stupid! I have time for friends and a relationship."

Is that true? I pause while I think about it. Working shifts, the evenings and weekends, the early mornings, I don't have as much free time at the same times that Matt does, sure, but I need more in my life then just a relationship. I need Zoe. I need a social life.

"Why would you let what he said stop you from talking to me though? Why wouldn't you just explain to me? You could have told me what he had said. We could have talked about it."

She's shaking her head. "No. No. You don't understand. I couldn't."

"Why the hell not? You just abandoned me! How do you think it felt? How do you think it feels to have the one person in life that you thought you could rely on just let you down like that?"

"I expect Luke might feel that about me too. That I've let him down. That I'm the one person he thought he could depend on. Look at me. Fuck." She puts her face into her hands. "What a mess."

"Does he know? How? What...? No. Tell me about Matt first."

"Of course, I felt awful not talking to you. I felt awful about how you must be feeling, and I felt absolutely terrible in myself that I couldn't talk to you. Every day I wanted to message you. When you came to the school...it took everything I had to not run down there to see you. I really thought I could get away with it, but I thought that somehow, he would find out. That he would know."

"Wait, what does this have to do with Matt?"

"He told me that I needed to back off and get out of your life. No messages. No contact."

"Then you should have told him to piss off, and then told me what he had said to you..."

Zoe is looking out of the window, or at least she would be if it hadn't fogged over. She's staring at the grey blankness when she speaks.

"He said that if I didn't break contact with you that he would tell Luke about Theo."

"Sorry, what?" I heard her. I know what she said, but it sounds so unlike Matt to threaten anyone like that, I need to hear it again.

"He said he would tell Luke about my *affair* if I didn't stop taking up your time." She spits that word 'affair' like it has a bad taste.

"Fuck, Zoe."

I don't know what else to say. My vast vocabulary singles out the basest of words and her name. That's all I have.

Now I sit in stunned silence.

"I'm so sorry for hurting you. I can't imagine what I would think if you vanished from my life like that. Do you understand why I had to do what Matt said?"

I nod slowly. The ghost cloud of condensation on the window runs with tiny rivulets.

"Are you not worried now? That he will know we have been talking? If you can come here today, why couldn't you come here before? Why couldn't you talk to me when I came to your work? He would never have known."

"I couldn't take the risk, Vi. Of course, it was *unlikely* he would find out, but I couldn't risk everything on that chance. I convinced myself that he had eyes everywhere. I was so paranoid. I'm sorry."

"Why now?" I ask again.

"Because now, it doesn't matter. I've told Luke."

I want to dive straight into this, find out what's happening, be there for Zoe, but I'm still completely dumbfounded by the revelation about Matt.

"How could Matt do that? Why? He never said anything to me…"

My mind jumps back to conversations I've had with Matt. Things he has said. *Let it go.*

"He…I didn't think he was like that. Was I so stupid?"

"I know that he's your boyfriend and everything, but all I really know about him is what he showed me of himself. He wanted me out of your life so that you could spend all your spare time with him. He wanted that so much that he thought nothing of threatening me. I believe he would have gone through with it, obviously, or I'd have just told him to go jump."

"I'm glad you're back Zoe. I'm glad you're here now. Okay, okay. What does this mean for you? What's happening with Luke?"

Zoe groans.

"It was the right thing to do," she says. "I couldn't keep lying to him. I thought that telling him would be the worst thing I've ever done, but instead, all I felt was relief."

"How did he take it?"

"He said that he knew something was going on. He sensed something different about me. But, get this, he didn't want to say anything because he thought I seemed happier than I had been for a long time, and he didn't want that to change."

"But when you told him about Theo? He can't have been happy about that!"

"Not *happy*, no. Of course not. But he's lived in the relationship just as much as I have. He knew that we were broken, even though neither of us wanted to address it. It's like we have both been play-acting and now, now that I've told him about Theo, there's this openness. We can finally talk about things."

"So, are you leaving him? Is he leaving you?"

"Actually, we are going to take a little time to think about what to do. Now that we are discussing things, it's like a blanket has been lifted. We can see what's underneath. I still love him. He still loves me. We are trying to work out whether we should stay together."

"And Theo?" I think about the gorgeous man who had been so kind and considerate.

"I don't know. That's part of what I have to work out. He's great. He's part of why I'm here with you now. After you met up with him, he told me how upset you were. I knew I couldn't carry on like that any longer. Hiding from Luke, keeping away from you. It's not the life I wanted."

"He seems lovely."

"And what about Luke?" she laughs. "You've always liked him well enough."

I look her straight in the eye. The rain sounds like tiny pebbles dropping on the car roof.

"I just want you to be happy, Zo. Whatever you choose, I'll be there."

She reaches over, pressing into the gearstick in an uncomfortable hunch, and hugs me.

I hold on to her like I've never been held before. Her warmth in the cold car, her scent, that familiar light rose. I don't ever want to let go.

When we break free, I say, "What am I going to do about Matt?"

CHAPTER TWENTY-SIX

I know that I have to confront Matt but, apart from that, I have no idea what to do next. I would never have believed that he could do something like this, but I believe Zoe, I trust her completely, and so I have to doubt Matt. Someone who is so controlling that he wanted my best friend out of my life can't be good for me. I think back to life with Adrian, and remember the obvious, unconcealed control. I laugh at the thought that enters my head: at least he was honest. Even if he was a complete asshole, he was honest. I knew what I was dealing with. The guy before Adrian. Him too. The same. I knew. I knew alright.

I could message Matt, have this out over text messaging, avoid the need to see him, but no. This is something that I have to do face-to-face. He's due to come over tonight anyway, so my plan is to launch straight into it. No sense putting it off. I couldn't stand to be around him, knowing his duplicity, trying to act like everything is fine when it's far from it.

He greets me at the door with his usual kiss, and I pull back. I step aside to let him through to the flat. I don't want him turning tail on the doorstep, avoiding the denouement. We get into the living room and sit. Him on the sofa, me on the armchair. He looks confused that I am not sitting next to him, and he's about to speak when I spit it out.

"I've spoken to Zoe."

As soon as I say the words, his face changes. He becomes a different person. He doesn't speak. He sits stock still, looking at me, as though waiting to see what I will do next. For some reason I think of a field mouse being stalked by an eagle, and I am just as timid in his sights. I don't know what to expect. I don't know how he will respond. I expected some kind of response though.

"I said…"

He holds up a flat palm, and I automatically flinch.

He pauses and watches me again, shaking his head.

We both sit, speechless, my four words hanging in the air.

Eventually, I have to say something.

"What were you thinking? Why would you –" I don't even know how to finish the sentence, so I shake my head. "Matt, seriously. I thought that we could have been something. We could have had something good. But this. This is crazy."

"Crazy?" he says. The word prompts a response, even if its only a repetition. "Crazy?"

"Think about it! You threatened Zoe! You pretty much blackmailed her into staying away from me. That's not normal behaviour." Even though I'm only wearing a dress and cardigan, I feel like I'm wearing too many layers of clothes. I'm hot and constricted, unable to relax. I'm upright on the edge of the chair, leaning in to him, poised.

"That's not how I meant it. I mean, I understand why it comes across that way…why you'd think…" Matt desperately fumbles for words. He runs his hands through his hair. It looks less endearing today, somehow, that rusty brown mess. He seems older, his eyes sunken, his cheeks sallow.

I stare, waiting for him to say something worth hearing.

He inhales deeply, and lets the breath out in a mouthy moan, and then begins to gush.

"You work all the time. When you're not at work, you're with her. How do you ever expect to have a relationship when you're not prepared to put in the time? You have to give as well as take. I'm not going to be there only when you have time for me. You have to compromise. You have to give some things up so that you can be happy."

"Happy? Have you even noticed how I've been? Have you listened to anything I've said to you? I've been worried sick about Zoe, and then frantically trying to find out what's happened with her. And you haven't even asked about work. I've been going through something awful and I don't even feel like I can talk about it with you. It's only been a few weeks...and you start off what you think could be a *happy* relationship by threatening my best friend and putting me through the stress and anxiety of making her vanish from my life"

As I speak the word *anxiety,* I realise that I'm not feeling at all anxious. There are none of the usual signs of an impending panic attack. Something about that thought gives me strength.

"How could you do that? Why would you do something so ridiculous?"

"Ridiculous? Ridiculous, am I?" He shifts forward in his chair, leans in towards me so that his face is only inches from mine. I gulp instinctively.

"You don't know anything about me. You don't know what it was like for me, growing up with my parents. You think you know my mother because you work with her? You think you know anything?"

My mind is a confused muddle. Matt and I are only a few weeks into our relationship. It's so new that it's barely a relationship at all. This has happened so quickly, too quickly. Zoe was right all along. I think about that conflict resolution course again. I am calm. I need to keep him calm. I don't want this to escalate.

"I don't know, no. I'm sorry. You've obviously had a very hard time."

I think about when I was Elizabeth, talking callers through stress, through suicidal thoughts, through times when they felt out of control. I think about midwife-me. Calm and professional. Solid and dependable. I think about what I've been through and what I've come through. I can deal with this.

"I'm sorry that your mother wasn't there with you or there for you."

He begins to lose the serrated edge that had crept in. He is dulling, recoiling, retreating.

"I only wanted to be with you. I wanted to spend time with you."

"I wanted that too. But what you did…it was wrong. You hurt me. And I can't keep spending time with you now." I pause to see what effect my words have, to check whether they have filtered through. "You understand that, don't you?"

He nods, childlike.

"There's no going back from this. I'm sorry, Matt," I say, and I mean it. I am sorry. I wish that this had worked out differently. I thought that at last something or someone good had come into my life, and all that's happened is that I've run into a variation on a theme. Matt. Adrian. The guy before Adrian. Line them up, shoot them down. All the same, all different but all the same.

"We can work something out. I'll apologise to Zoe. Whatever you want, just say it. I take all of the blame. You're great, Vi. You really are great. Everything was my fault. Everything."

He's right, of course, but that doesn't matter. I think about Zoe's face when she told me about what Matt had done. I think about the past couple of weeks. I have needed Zoe and she couldn't be there for me because of the man that is sitting on my sofa, asking for a second chance when all I can think about really is how soon I can get him out of my flat and have the night to myself.

"Matt, I can't. You have to go. I'm sorry. It's over." I'm not sure that I'm sorry at all. The more I think about it, the more sure I am that I'm not sorry. I am calm, I am in control. I feel confident. I say goodbye.

After Matt has left, I do what any girl in that situation would do. I do what I have always done. I text Zoe.

It's over. I've finished with Matt. Feel surprisingly good xx

This time, her return message pings up quickly.

Glad you're okay. Sorry it ended like this. Do you need anything? xx

When Zoe asks if I need anything, I interpret it so differently than I did when Matt asked if I needed anything. Zoe's question is supportive, caring, attentive, not suggestive. I know that if there is anything that I need she would bring it. Physical or emotional. I know that she is there for me. I know that she is back.

CHAPTER TWENTY-SEVEN

The next day, I get another message from Matt.

I was an idiot. I'm so sorry. xx

Just that. He doesn't ask for a second chance, he doesn't beg for forgiveness, he apologises. It throws me a little. I'm not sure how to reply. Am I meant to tell him that it's okay? Do I accept his sorry sorry? Do I ignore him? I know what it feels like to be ignored, and I don't wish it upon anyone, not even him. I can't hold on to bitterness, even after what he made me go through. I feel sorry for him. Sorry. Such a simple, complicated word.

I accept your apology, but please don't message me again.

It feels like I'm being terribly harsh, but I don't have any desire to talk to him. I want to be clear. I want it to be final. I don't think about my words any further, I click send, and under my breath I say, "Goodbye."

I soon get back into my routine of working shifts, seeing Zoe, enjoying me-time. I check in on Claire every few days and follow her progress. Two weeks after her Caesarean she has surgery to remove the tumour from her spine. The growth turns out to be entirely enclosed within the dural sac, the space around the spine, and Doctor Harrison, Sherrie, is confident that it's been removed completely. Claire will need to stay on ward seven to recover, and then come back to the hospital for follow up scans. It's the beginning of a long journey, but it looks like the destination is a positive one.

One Monday afternoon, after my shift, and before I head to Coffee Express to meet Zoe, I pop in to visit Claire. I press the intercom button and the nurse at the desk replies. As soon as she clocks that it's me, she buzzes me through.

"Hi Violet," she says, as I stop at the desk.

Rachel offers me a chocolate from the large red tub on the desk, and I accept. I try to avoid having too many on the maternity ward, but when I come down here, I let myself have a treat sometimes. Besides, they have the Galaxy caramels, and I'm a sucker for their sticky sweetness.

"Is Claire okay for visitors?" I ask, before sticking the chocolate in my mouth.

She nods. "She's been awake about ten minutes. She's still very tired, but she'll be glad to see you."

"Is Michael here?"

"Not right now, no."

"Ladies afternoon it is then."

I smile and carry on down the corridor to Claire's side room.

She's upright, reading a book, but doesn't notice me straight away.

"Hi," I say. "How's things?"

"Oh hi, Violet." She puts the book onto her bedside cabinet without bothering to mark the page.

I walk over and give her a gentle hug. It's four days since she had her tumour removed, and she's going to be tender for a while yet. She's going to be needing pain relief for some time, but Sherrie is optimistic about her prognosis, and so is Claire.

"They're letting Libby out of the neonatal unit today!" Her thoughts first upon her baby, before she even considers telling me about her own feelings.

"That's great. She's done so well."

Claire isn't smiling.

"Oh. She's going home with Michael?"

Claire nods, lips trembling, her eyes welling with tears that she's desperately trying not to spill. It's like trying to hold water in a full bucket when you're running. Impossible.

"I'm sorry," I say. It's all I can say. What else is there?

"I dreamed of the day that Michael and I would take our baby home from the hospital together but now she's going home, and I'm stuck in this bed, attached to all these machines and tubes. So many drugs that I've forgotten the name of most of them. Stitches down my spine. I can't get comfortable no matter how I lie. And the nausea. Even with all the…" She pauses to give me the technical term for anti-sickness medication. "Antiemetics. Even with those. I feel sick all the time. I'm not myself. I can't do anything. I can't be a mother."

The heart rate monitor beeps furiously at us.

"Claire please, I know you're having a terrible time. I can't begin to imagine what it's like for you, but I can see how distressed you are. I'm so sorry you're having to go through this. Right now, though, try to relax a little for me." I think about my panic attacks, my fainting episodes, the way my body fails to respond to my commands, and I wonder how effective I could possibly expect it to be, telling Claire to relax.

She looks over at the machine with its red digital readout. The little, frequent pulses.

"I know. I know," she says and exhales softly.

I sit on the edge of the bed, trying to hold her hand without dislodging the IV line.

"Violet. Thank you for visiting me. I know it's not part of your job to be here. It means a lot to me."

I wave the thank you away as unnecessary.

"Life's too short, you know. I've learned that. That's what I'm taking from this. Whatever happens to me now. Life's too short. I feel like I've wasted so much of it. We waited to get married, we waited to have a baby, perhaps I've used up all of the time I had. Wasted it waiting for the right time. The right time…it's now, isn't it? For whatever you want to do."

I feel like she's trying to give me a message, like a gift wrapped in ribbon, mine to take and cherish.

I think about Matt, and how I rushed into our relationship without thinking carefully enough, without knowing enough about him to work out whether it was the right thing to do. I think about how I'd planned to do things for myself, to get to know myself, to be free. I try to work out how her advice fits in with my experiences. It feels so right but living in the moment hasn't always served me so well.

"And Violet, hold on to the ones you love. Tell them every day. Hold them tightly."

I nod. This is something I have no trouble agreeing to. I've felt what life is like without Zoe. I don't want to ever feel that again. What if this were me? Or her? Claire is so strong; could I be that way?

"You can get through this. You can still live your life. You and Michael and Libby. You'll be together. You'll be out of here before you know it, and this," I indicate the room, the hospital, the trauma she is currently going through, all with one sweep of my hand. "This will be nothing but a memory."

I feel like I'm speaking in shallow sentiments, but I don't know what else to say.

She's about to reply when the door opens behind me and Rachel pops her head in.

"I have a couple more visitors for you, Claire," she says with a grin that can only mean one thing.

The door swings open and Michael clumsily walks in, carrying a car seat in which Libby is sitting, covered in a soft fluffy blanket, eyes wide open, looking at her mum. Her big blue eyes fix on Claire as soon as Michael is close enough.

I've been the plus one to so many parent-infant interactions, but I know, right at the moment, as it's happening, that this is one that will stay with me. I can almost feel the endorphins that must be pumping through Claire's system as Michael lifts Libby and places her in Claire's arms.

When I walk out of Claire's room, I almost collide with Sherrie. She's bustling down the corridor, looking down into a Manilla record folder, her glasses perched

314

precariously at the end of her nose. I haven't seen her since things ended with her son, but I've always known that eventually I would. I think for a split second about ducking behind her, trying to avoid confrontation, but she stops and looks at me.

"Didn't work out with Matt?" she says, all matter-of-fact.

"Um, no. It's difficult with shifts…" I say, and trail off, hoping that she will understand and that this will be enough.

"So he said. I did warn him not to get involved with doctors or nurses." She says it with a smile, as though she's sharing some kind of inside joke with me, rather than telling me that she had told her son not to see me. Perhaps it is a joke. I don't know how to take it.

"Or midwives," I say, but she has me tagged as a nurse anyway, so the semantics don't matter. "He's a…" I think about what words to use. "Really interesting man. I'm sorry I wasn't the one."

Sherrie brushes it away. "He is interesting. Yes. Sometimes things just don't work out. I dare say you will both live to love another day. No harm done."

No harm done. Is that true? I had the two weeks of misery and stress wondering where my best friend was and what had happened to make her not want to talk to me. I had worry and anxiety and sadness, and all of that was caused by Matt. Zoe lived in fear of Matt telling Luke about her and Theo. She had her own stress caused by Matt too. But somehow, we have both, Zoe and I, come out of the other side of this somehow changed for the better. We know what it is like to be apart and we never want to experience that again. More than that, though. I have learned that I can stand up to a man and close down a relationship that is negative. I have done that without having an anxiety attack, and for that I am proud. Zoe found the courage to talk to Luke about their relationship, and admitted her affair. Nothing excuses Matt's behaviour, but here I stand, less anxious, more confident.

"No harm done," I say.

EPILOGUE

The day of the gin festival comes around before we know it. Zoe and I have planned our outfits, set out a schedule for how much we will allow ourselves to drink through the day, and have made a pact to not let each other do or say anything stupid. Despite our best efforts, by six pm, we are sitting on two swings, rocking slowly, putting the world to rights.

I kick my legs forward, pull them inwards, and propel myself back and forwards, enjoying the freedom, but beginning to feel the creeping edge of nausea.

"Slow down, Vi," Zoe says. She's got her heels dug into the ground, and is using her weight against them to move the swing oh-so-slightly.

"I'm starting to feel a bit –" I slow myself down, dragging my feet across the floor, trying to keep my lunch down. "A bit sick," I say as I come to a stop next to her.

"Gin and swinging might just be a mistake, Vi."

"I've made a lot of mistakes," I say. It's so much of an understatement that it could even be an under-understatement.

"Matt. Adrian. C…"

She's about to say his name. The guy before Adrian. The guy we don't talk about.

"Carl," I say. I've named him. There. Isn't there some superstition that says when you name someone they stop having power over you? In this case it's the other way around. I don't feel like he has any power over me anymore, so I can name him.

"Wow," Zoe says. She knows the significance of this moment. "Well done you." She bends in, tugging on the chains that support her, and hugs me through the cold metal. I have no tension. I am soft, I am relaxed.

I've not had a single panic attack since I've been on my own. I feel like something has changed inside me.

"Maybe you just needed some time to be you. To breathe."

"Well you could have told me that before I started seeing Matt," I say, poking her gently in the

318

ribs. I take a big breath of the outdoors air. Today I feel free. I feel alive.

"I did tell you!" she protests, and then realises that I'm joking with her. "Let the records show that today on the event of the gin festival, I did advise that you should remain single for…a long time."

"That's very specific. I agree. I will not date anyone for a long time."

"And, let the records also state that no stupid man…"

"Or woman…"

"Okay, or woman…no stupid person shall ever come between us again. We are Ziolet. We are Voe. We are…"

"We are pissed."

As is often the way with Zoe and I, we collapse, quite literally, off the swings in a fit of giggles. We could just as easily be the seven-year-old girls that we were when we used to swing here years ago. If we weren't so drunk, that is.

By ten to midnight, we are sitting on the quayside, sharing a bench, sharing a final plastic cup of elderflower gin. We've said our drunken *I love yous* and visited the Porta-Potties many times, without a repeat of Knickergate. It's time to go home.

The car pulls up beside us and Zoe squeals.

"Here he is! You're not going to chuck up in there are you? Promise."

"I'm fine," I slur, not at all fine.

"Ladies," he says as he steps out, and opens the rear door for me.

Zoe leaps to give him a sloppy drunken kiss and he laughs, embracing her.

"Hi Luke," I say. I slump into the seat, wondering whether I would be better lying down, curling up.

I wind down the window, let in the air. The breeze is sweet against my skin. Zoe and Luke are still holding each other, standing beside the car. She's whispering something into his ear but all I can see is his beaming response.

Zoe and Luke. Claire and Michael. Everyone faces their own obstacles in their own ways. I might be alone now, but perhaps that's what I need to be for a while.

Zoe pushes open the other rear door, tumbles into the back seat next to me and rests her drunken head onto my lap.

"Take us home, driver," she says, slurring every word.

I'm not alone. I'm never alone. Never again.

Made in the USA
Coppell, TX
19 June 2024